How to Charm an Earl

How to Charm an Earl

LADY BE SEDUCTIVE
BOOK ONE

DAWN BROWER

"The Very first moment I beheld him, my heart was irrevocably gone."

— JANE AUSTEN, LOVE AND
FRIENDSHIP

Contents

EXCERPT: THE WALLFLOWER IDENTITY

EXCERPT: ROGUE WALLFLOWER

EXCERPT: HER DUKE TO SAVOR

EXCERPT: HER DUKE OF SIN

EXCERPT: HER DUKE TO
SAVOR

Take time to enjoy what gives you pleasure, even if to some it might be considered sinful.

Lady Athena Thompson stared at the treasure chest located in the attic. She had never seen anything more beautiful in her entire life. It was a rich mahogany with gold filigree, and it was covered in a layer of dust. The box was bigger than a jewelry chest, so it would hold more than precious baubles.

"What do you think is inside it?" her twin sister, Maeve, asked. They were mirror twins. They each had hair as dark as the night sky and ice-blue eyes, but where they differed was where their dimples were placed, and they each only had one. It was a little eerie... Athena's was on her left cheek, and Maeve's on her right. That was how the servants had been able to tell them apart. Somehow their father knew even if the dimple wasn't visible how to tell the twins apart.

"There is only one way to find out," Isla, their older sister by two years, said. "We need to open it."

"But it has a lock on it," Athena said. "How are we going to do that?"

Isla grinned. "Leave that to me," she told them.

She pulled a pin out of her hair and bent it a little, then placed it in the lock on the chest. Isla tilted her head to the side and leaned it closer to the box. It seemed as if she was listening for something... Then she grinned and twisted the pin. "There you are," she said, beaming. "Unlock now, you little beastie."

Athena frowned. Her sister could be a little odd at times, but this was...definitely leaning toward beyond strange. "Are you talking to the lock?"

"And if I am?" Isla lifted her brow, daring her to say the wrong thing.

Maeve giggled. Athena lifted her hands and said, "I mean nothing by it. I don't know how to pick a lock. I'm only curious."

What she didn't say, and probably should have, was to remind her sister that everyone already stared at them as if they were odd creatures. It had a lot to do with how they looked, but even more to do with their family's history. All three of them got their appearances from their mother—from their dark hair right down to their ice-blue eyes. Somewhere along the way in their family line, that coloring had bred true. Their father was blond and had blue eyes, but his eyes were darker in color than theirs.

Many believed they descended from witches. One of their ancestors, John Alden, had been accused of witchcraft in Salem in the seventeenth century. He had been acquitted, but that stigma had followed him. Their mother was an Alden and her family still resided in Boston. Their American roots were another check against them as far as the ton was concerned.

The lock clicked, and Isla lifted the lid on the box. They all leaned over it and peered inside. "Is that a book?" Maeve asked.

"It is," Isla said and pulled it out. She flipped open the cover and read the first page. "The Diary of Sybil Alden," she said quietly. "Was this mother's before she wed father?"

Athena swallowed the lump that had formed in her throat. None of them truly knew their mother. She had died giving birth to her and Maeve. Isla had her for two years, but even she was too young to remember her. All they had were tales her father told them, and some stories from their grandfather Jack when he came over from Boston. They didn't get too many visits from him either...

"I want to read it," Athena said. "Let me see it."

Isla clutched it to her chest. "No," she said. "What I mean is..." She sighed. "We all should have a turn with it in private. This is something that we will all treasure and we shouldn't fight over it. None of us want to accidentally damage it, do we?"

Athena and Maeve both shook their heads. "You're right," Athena said. "How do we decide who reads it first?"

"First, let's see what else is in the chest." Isla glanced down. "There is more than this diary inside."

They all huddled around the chest once more. There were some trinkets inside. Three to be exact... They were pendants. Each had a gold chain with a small black stone attached with a gold initial embedded in it. The first letter of each of their names. "Do you think mother meant for us to have these?"

"But how would she have known..." Isla frowned. "She didn't know you two would be girls..."

She was right. They hadn't been born when their mother had died, yet here were three pendant that were designed for them. "What should we do?"

"I think we should keep the pendant with our respective initials on them," Maeve said. "I want it."

Isla grinned. "Then you shall have it." She handed Maeve the stone with a clear M embedded in it, then handed Athena the one with her own initial. "We should wear them."

"I agree," Maeve said.

Athena stared at her own pendant. She wasn't certain she wished to wear hers, but they might question her reluctance. "What about the diary?" she asked instead. "Do you want it first, Isla? Since you're the oldest?"

She shook her head. "No," she told Athena. "I think it should start with you, since technically you're the youngest. I have no wish to marry, but I know you do. Perhaps there is some useful insight in these pages that will guide you."

Maeve wrinkled her nose. "I'm too young to marry."

They were both eighteen. Their birthday had just passed a month earlier and their father had decided it was time for their debut ball in the next couple of months. They would return to London after the season was in full swing. In late April, their London townhouse would be opened and they would take up residence there. They would have all of March and a couple of weeks in April left in the country before they departed. Maeve would have been happy to remain out of society. Athena didn't blame her. No one seemed to like them; however, she wanted to fall in love. She couldn't very well do that if she remained cloistered in her family home.

"There is no rush for any of us to find husbands," Isla told her. "Enjoy your season."

"Did you enjoy your debut?" Maeve asked.

Isla glanced away. "Society isn't for everyone." Her tone was quiet, but the pain in her voice was unmistakable. "That doesn't mean it won't be special for the two of you." She had pasted a smile on her face, but Athena saw through it. She wouldn't push, though. If Isla wished to talk about it, she would.

Instead, she lifted her hand. "I will take the diary first." She wanted to know more about her mother, and this was her only chance to do so. "And then I'll give it to Maeve when I'm finished."

Maeve grinned. "I hope she had more than advice about love. Do you think it's true?"

"What is true?" Isla asked.

"That she was a witch." She glanced at Isla as if she'd grown another head, and that was a silly question to ask.

Isla frowned. "Of course not. Don't be ridiculous. Witchcraft isn't real."

This was an old argument. One that would never be resolved...or would it? Athena glanced down at the diary. There was only one way to find out, and she'd start reading about it later that night. "Let's go back to the sitting room. Someone will notice we're missing soon and father told us not to come up here."

"She's correct," Isla said, then stood. "Time to be respectable young ladies again." They all scurried out of the attic and headed back to the sitting room. They were all seated when the door opened and the housekeeper pushed in the tea cart. All three of them blew out a sigh of relief. They'd returned just in time.

Athena stared at the diary sitting on the table next to her and then ran her fingers over the black pendant. What did this all mean? Would she find the answers in that diary, and would she be happy with what she did discover?

One

One month later...

Restlessness rolled over Athena in waves... She'd had her mother's journal for weeks now and she still hadn't read one page. She was surprised that neither of her sisters had asked for it yet. Were they not eager to read it too? More importantly why hadn't she devoured every word her mother had written already? Why was she so terrified to start reading?

Because once she finished it, she'd no longer have something to look forward to from her mother... She hadn't wanted to admit that to herself. Perhaps it was time to let that go and open the journal. Not here though... She couldn't stay inside another moment longer.

"Why are you pacing, sister dear," Maeve asked as she entered the sitting room. "The last time you fretted, you were so afraid father wouldn't let you buy that horse you favored."

She did love that horse... "True," Athena answered. "But I had good reason. Hades has a terrible temperament with the grooms. I feared father wouldn't allow me to ride him. Even though he's a complete sweetheart."

Maeve rolled her eyes. "That horse is a nuisance."

"Don't be a grump," Athena told her sister. "He has excellent taste and loves me."

"And he hates me," Maeve said. "We're identical twins. How can he even tell us apart?"

"Perhaps he's noticed your dimple is on the other cheek." Athena shrugged and barely held back a grin. "Or that you're horrid with horses. Looks aren't everything."

"I don't even want to know what you are implying." Her sister sat down on the settee and leaned back against it. "Tell me what is bothering you now. We both know it has nothing to do with your wretched horse."

Should she tell her sister why she'd been pacing? Would Maeve even understand? She probably would. Neither of them had even had a chance to know their mother, and while Isla had two years with her, she couldn't remember anything. They all had a hole in their lives that would never be filled. That journal might give them something, but it couldn't replace their mother. "I am considering going for a ride."

"You're deflecting," Maeve said. "That's all right. You don't have to tell me." She tapped her head. "I bet I already know what is going on inside that head of yours."

"You can certainly try." Athena sighed. "But you've never been very good at reading my mind." She barely held back a grin. They had a bond that went beyond being just sisters. They had always been able to read each other's emotions, but telepathy was not in their wheelhouse.

"You're correct, of course," Maeve agreed. "But in this I think I am right." She leaned over and tapped the journal Athena had set on a nearby table. "This is what's troubling you. Did you read something disturbing that mother wrote?" She sat back up and met Athena's gaze. "Is that why you're pacing?"

Athena shook her head. "I haven't read anything yet."

Her sister gasped. "You've had it a month," her sister exclaimed. "Why the blazes not?'

Perhaps her sister didn't understand as she thought she might... "Because..." How the hell did she explain it? "Once I finish it..."

"There won't be anything else left," Maeve supplied, then nodded. "I do understand. I just hadn't considered it because it isn't my time with the journal. Perhaps when I do have it, I will take my time as well."

She should never have doubted her sister. Maeve had always understood her, even when others didn't. They had gone to finishing school for a year, but only one. Not because they wouldn't have benefitted from extra learning, but because the other students were horrid. They had begged their father to let them return home and have tutors instead. With their ancestry, many looked at them as less than they were. It didn't matter that their father was an earl. Society only considered that their mother was an American, and not even one they deemed acceptable. Money had nothing to do with it either. Her mother's family had made a lot of that in shipping and other merchant endeavors. They were far wealthier than their father's family had ever been. They had, and always would be, outsiders. Which was why Isla had given up on the idea of marriage and resigned herself to spinsterhood. That may very well be Athena's and Maeve's paths as well. But they wanted to at least try before giving in.

"I do think I am going to go for that ride," Athena said, then picked up the journal. "Perhaps I'll find a nice sunny location to start reading."

Maeve grinned. "Hades will be glad to see you. He's a beast, but he is yours."

"That he is," Athena agreed. Her horse was one devilish monster. The breeder hadn't thought he would be appropriate for a woman rider, and honestly, a normal lady would have been too tame for a horse as large as Hades. Athena did not ride sidesaddle. She had riding breeches designed for her so she could be astride her horse as he galloped through the fields. Skirts only got in the way... "And he needs exercise daily. I should see to that at the very least."

"Well, you enjoy your ride." Maeve stood. "And I'll go to my studio. I am working on a spectacular landscape. When it's finished, I think it'll make a nice gift."

"For who?" Athena asked.

"I don't know yet," Maeve answered honestly. "I just know it is meant for someone. Perhaps I have not met who it is intended for yet." Her sister had a faraway look on her face, as if she was seeing some distant future. She shook her head and then met Athena's gaze. "Either way, I'll show it to you once I've finished. Go for your ride now. We both have things to do."

Athena laughed and exited the sitting room. Her sister was rude, but that did not make her wrong. They both did have their tasks, and she was going to see to hers...

ROMAN JAMES, the Earl of Kendal, rode along his friend the Duke of Thornridge's property. He'd come to the duke's country house because he had needed time to recuperate from his injuries during Waterloo, but hadn't wanted to return to his own home. His mother would have had a fit if she'd realized how close Roman had come to dying. His injuries had been grave, and it had taken him months to recover enough to travel, then he'd settled in at Thornridge Castle. He'd been there for three months now, and he should return home soon, but he couldn't bring himself to leave. While he had been in his sick bed, he'd learned of his older brother's death.

That had been more of a shock than he'd wanted to admit...

Roman was never meant to be the earl. He'd been all right with his lot in life. He'd become a soldier and had intended to live his life as one. His brother Cassius was the perfect son. Their father had groomed him to take over the title and practically ignored Roman. In fact, Roman preferred when he did ignore him. His life was much easier that way. For him, it was a blessing when their father died suddenly. It had freed him from what little constraints he'd had in his life. Cassius had encouraged him to purchase his commission.

But neither of them had expected Cassius would die in a similar way as their father... They both had taken ill suddenly, and succumbed to that illness. Then Roman had almost died, too. Thankfully, he still breathed, but that was labored. Something his mother wouldn't fail to notice. Hence his sojourn with the Duke of Thornridge, his oldest friend. He hadn't even told his mother he had returned to

England. It was best to wait until he was more himself. Each day he breathed a little easier and winced less with pain. His side ached whenever he took too deep of a breath and his thigh itched with pain where he'd been slashed clear to the bone.

Today was one of the better days. He'd felt decent enough that a ride didn't seem impossible. That didn't mean he didn't have any pain, just that it had been more bearable. Maybe one day he'd be able to move without feeling slices of agony ripping through him, but it was yet to happen. He sighed and pulled on the reins. He needed a slight break to catch his breath. Roman closed his eyes and sucked in a bit of air, then released it. When he opened his eyes, he thought he might be seeing things.

A blur raced by him. Roman would swear it was a woman on one of the largest horses he'd ever seen. Her black hair was loose and flowing down in waves, whipping in the wind as she urged her horse on. What surprised him the most was her clothing. Had she been wearing breeches? He blinked several times before his muddled thoughts caught up to him. Roman had to know more about her. He flipped the rein and urged the horse to a gallop. That was perhaps more than his battered body could bear, but he couldn't find any reason to care as he settled in for the horse's breakneck speed.

She had quite the head start on him, but he was determined to locate her. Luckily for him she had slowed down by a nearby pond. Her horse stopped by the pond and she slid off her saddle, then tied the reins to a nearby post. How often had she come to this pond? It was on Thornridge's land, and he wondered if the duke knew he had a regular trespasser. He'd wandered enough of the ducal estate to have become familiar with the landscape.

Roman slowed his own horse to a walk. He didn't want to startle the girl. She was pulling a blanket out of one of her saddlebags and a small sack. A meal perhaps? She laid the blanket down and then reached into the sack. She presented something from within it to her horse as she stroked his mane.

He moved closer and he could hear her mumbling something, but the words were not decipherable. Roman cleared his throat, and it startled her, then the horse in succession. She lifted her hand to her chest. "Sir," she said in a scolding tone. "You should not sneak up on a person. It's quite rude."

Roman held back a smile. "My apologies," he told her. "That was not my intention."

She lifted her brow. "And what exactly are your intentions?" Her glare was enough to flay a man. It was too bad she didn't realize it wouldn't take much to completely do him in or she might not be so hard on him. Her gorgeous mouth was full, but clearly, she would not be inviting him to kiss her. That in itself was a pity. "Or do you even know what you hope to gain by accosting me?"

"Now that's going a bit far, don't you think?" It was his turn to lift a brow. "It is quite difficult to accost anyone when one hasn't even had time to dismount." Though to be fair, he'd done his fair share of damage to some soldiers in the war from atop his horse. He had been in the Cavalry, after all. But she did not know that, and he didn't have a saber or weapon of any kind on his person.

"I suppose that is true." She narrowed his gaze. "You don't appear to have ill intentions, but as I have never been introduced to you, how am I to know what you wish from me?"

She was so bloody lovely it ached to look at her. Her dark hair looked luscious, and he wanted to stroke his fingers over those thick tresses. Why had she left it unbound for her ride? And he'd already studied those lips of hers... Her eyes were an eerie ice-blue that seemed to pierce right through him. He had to know more about her. "I am Lord Kendal," he said. "I'm visiting His Grace, the Duke of Thornridge. It is his land you're riding over."

The woman smiled at him. "Is it?" Her lips twitched a little. "It's a pleasure to make your acquaintance, my lord." She picked up her blanket and folded it neatly and replaced it in her saddlebag along with her little sack. "Then I suppose I should return to my family's land. I would hate to trespass." With liquid grace, she hopped back onto her saddle. He was amazed at her skill, and a little dumbstruck at the view of her rear in those breeches. Women should never wear breeches. It was enough to make a man lose his mind.

"You're leaving," he said when she pulled her horse's reins firmly into her hands.

"Yes," she said. "Isn't that why you approached me? To warn me that I was on the duke's land?"

"No," he told her. "I really don't give a damn why you're here."

Her lips twitched. "That is good to know, my lord." Her eyes seemed to dance with mischief. "Perhaps we will meet again someday." She nodded at him. "Until then," she began. "Enjoy your stay at the duke's estate. I hear he's a beast of a man and hard to be around. I'd hate to be his guest."

With those words, she flicked the reins and galloped away. It wasn't until she was out of sight that he realized he'd never gained her name. He'd been a bloody idiot. But that didn't matter. She was Thornridge's neighbor. How many beautiful women could possibly live on the estate next to the duke's?

Two

Athena dismounted Hades and then led him to the stables and secured him to a nearby post. She kept his attention on her as a stable hand removed his saddle and other tack. After everything was taken off she led him to his stall. She removed his harness and handed it to the stable hand.

"Bring me a brush," she told the stable hand. Hades had been wonderful and ridden as hard as she'd demanded. Athena wanted to reward him for being the best horse she'd ever owned. The stable hand brought her the brush, and she groomed him. Athena brushed and brushed him and he practically preened before her. "You're wonderful," she told

Hades. "The bestest horse that ever was a horse." She sounded like an idiot, but Athena didn't care.

After she finished brushing him, she exited the stall and closed the gate, then pushed the lock into place. She couldn't allow Hades to escape because none of the stable hands could handle him if she wasn't around to keep him calm. That was one of the reasons her father had been reluctant to allow her to have Hades. He was an unruly horse, and he hadn't wanted to risk Athena's safety. She reached into a nearby bag and pulled out a sugar cube and gave it to Hades. He crunched it and let out a ninny of appreciation. "You're perfect," she reassured Hades. "I'd spend more time with you if I could, but I must go inside now."

She still had read nothing in her mother's diary. That had been her intention when she'd gone for her ride. Athena had planned on settling down by the pond and reading the first few pages, but that had changed when Lord Kendal had made his appearance. It hadn't felt like the right time to open the journal and read her mother's words. Not with such a handsome and alluring man catching all of her attention.

That was when she knew she had to leave. He was a temptation she hadn't planned on, and it scared her to her very soul. Athena had never met anyone that had sparked her attention so quickly. She was restless in nature and prone to pacing to rid herself of excess anxiety. Sitting still in a serene pose was foreign to her. Maeve could occasionally, but it was their oldest sister, Isla, that had the calmness that soothed everyone around them. Athena would never be that type of woman. So it had unnerved her to realize she could focus all of her attention on one man and have it calm her so effectively. She had to discuss it with her sisters.

Athena placed a quick kiss on Hades' mane and then said, "I'll be back tomorrow. I promise." She always kept her promises, especially to her horse. When they went to London, he would remain behind and that would be hell for the stable hands. They'd have to let him loose in the paddock so he got some exercise because no one else could ride him.

With a sigh, she stepped away from his stall and exited the stables. She made her way to the house and went to her bedchamber. As much as she wanted to speak to at least one of her sisters, she had to change out of her riding gear first. Her father frowned at her wearing breeches and didn't like to see her in them. He wouldn't go so far as to forbid her wearing them as long as they were at Harwood Hall. Being the daughter of the Earl of Harwood had some advantages, even if society thought they were ill bred mongrels.

She reached her bedchamber and stepped inside. Her maid was already waiting for her. "Mary," she greeted. "I need to change quickly. Is my gown ready?" Mary knew her well and should have prepared for her arrival, but Athena usually took her time changing.

"Yes, my lady," Mary said. "Your gown is pressed and ready for you. Your father requested you stop by his study when you returned for your ride. I think he wishes to speak with all three of you."

What could her father wish to discuss with them that required such urgency? She blew out a breath and turned toward Mary. "Then we best hurry. I've probably kept him waiting longer than he wished."

She quickly stripped her clothes off and handed them to Mary to launder. Athena only had a few pairs of breeches and she wanted to keep them in the best condition as possible. It was quite difficult for a woman to have them made. Seamstresses were appalled and men's tailors flat out refused. She always had several pairs made at once when she found someone willing to humor her request.

Mary helped her into her underclothes and then into her gown. It was a soft blue that was a shade darker than her eyes. Athena thought it brought out that color and she liked to enhance their beauty—even if most found them odd. She loved the color. Mainly because of the one portrait that existed of her mother. They got their coloring from her, from her dark hair to her light blue eyes. They were truly their mother's daughters.

"There," Mary said. "Now let's fix your hair. Why did you insist on taking it down before your ride? It's a tangled mess. It'll take a while to comb out all those knots."

Truly, she hadn't known why she wanted her hair down. Athena knew it was a bad idea, but she felt it had to be done. After her encounter with Lord Kendal, she couldn't help wondering if somehow she'd known she'd meet him and wanted him to see it down. Had he liked her hair?

She had certainly liked him. He was handsome and seemed to be kind. Athena wanted to know more about him, and it wasn't all about his dark hair and piercing gray eyes. He had tried to hide it, but it had been clear to her he'd been in pain. What had happened to him? "Try your best," Athena told

Mary. "I'll not complain as you brush them out. I promise."

Mary nodded and set to work and Athena became lost in thought. She couldn't wait to tell Isla and Maeve about the duke's visitor. Isla would hate him on principle. Her feelings for the duke were well known. Once upon a time she'd thought herself in love with him, but he'd broken her heart. Surely Lord Kendal wasn't a cad like the duke, but she couldn't be certain. Either way, she wanted to find out.

ROMAN SLID off of horse and winced as pain shot through him. He'd been out too long and would have to rub down his leg later. Otherwise, the muscles would stiffen and he'd be in even more pain later. He wished he had someone he trusted to do it for him, but there was no one he could rely on. It was up to him to see to his needs. He was the earl now and couldn't let anyone see him as weak.

He kept his pace slow as he headed toward Thornridge Castle. The duke would be in his study. That was where he spent most of his time. There was a lot involved in running a dukedom, and

Roman did not envy his friend. Roman had never wanted a title, and certainly not one as lofty as a duke. Being an earl would be a tremendous responsibility too, but nowhere near as suffocating as a duke.

The castle might be considered gloomy to some, but Roman had always liked it. Even when he had visited as a boy. Roman had attended Eton with Thornridge and they had become good friends there. The duke had been a duke even then. His parents had both died when he was only five years old. He'd been raised by an aunt and solicitors. His melancholy nature had been ever present. There was sadness in his eyes even now. Roman wished he could erase that for him, but he didn't know what would or could make Thornridge happy.

He reached the study and rapped on the doorframe to catch Thornridge's attention. "I know you're busy," he began. "You're always busy. But I had hoped I could entice you to take a break and assist me."

Thornridge set his quill down as he met Roman's gaze. He smiled, but it didn't reach his forever somber golden eyes. "What can I do for you?"

Roman had always known two things in life. He was a forever disappointment to his father, and

Thornridge would always be his friend. One he couldn't change, and the other he hoped never would. At least with his father's death, he could set the first aside. "I went riding earlier."

The duke's brow rose. "Was that wise?"

He grinned. "Perhaps not," he rubbed his aching thigh as he spoke. "But I had to try. I went farther this time than I have in the past." He'd kept to around the castle grounds when he attempted to get on a horse. This time he was determined to explore more of Thornridge land. He had visited in the past, but he had never gone far. There had been no reason to, and that was perhaps why he'd never seen her.

"I hope it was worth it." What he didn't say was that the pain would be unbearable later. Roman knew that better than his friend did. "You never said why you need my help."

"I made it as far as a pond on the east side of your property," he told the duke.

"I wouldn't recommend swimming there," the duke told him. "At least not for a few more months. Early April, it will be cold enough to freeze your bollocks off." His lips twitched. "Was that what you wished to know?"

Roman grinned. "No," he told his friend. "But that is good to know. I don't think it is wise to attempt swimming with my leg so unreliable. I might end up drowning if there is no one around to save me." And he rather liked his bollocks attached to his body, thank you very much. He'd rather they didn't freeze off. "I met someone there."

Thornridge stilled and slowly sat back against his chair. "Who?" His voice had gone gruff and, for the first time in his life, his eyes had an unfamiliar emotion rolling through them. Was that...anger? Heartbreak? He didn't quite understand what he was seeing. Did Thornridge have feelings for the hellion Roman had met?

"I'm not certain," he began slowly. "She never gave me her name. The only thing I can say with certainty is she lives nearby. I think the estate is near yours."

"I see." Thornridge glanced away. "There are three young ladies on that estate. It could be any of them, and they all look similar. Two are in fact identical..." He sighed. "It's been a few years since I've encountered any of them. I tend to stay in London." He rubbed his hands over his face, but didn't explain further.

Roman tilted his head to the side. "I didn't realize you don't reside here much when I asked for your help hiding my condition from my mother."

Thornridge had always loved his home. What would make him stay away?

"It's a long story," he said. "A tale I don't wish to expound upon."

"I understand," he said, but he didn't. Roman could only guess at to the reason, and it had to include one of those three ladies. But which one? He prayed it wasn't the one he'd suddenly become fascinated with. "What are their names?"

Thornridge swallowed hard. "Lady Athena and Lady Maeve are the twins," he answered. "The oldest sister is Lady Isla."

Had it been his imagination, or had his voice grown a little gruffer at the mention of Lady Isla? Had something happened between them? He didn't want to pry, but his curiosity had grown exponentially. It was best to leave his friend alone. His questions had left him anxious, and that had not been Roman's intention. "Thank you," he told Thornridge. "I'm sure you have much more work to do." He gestured toward the account books. "I'll see you at dinner. I have to see to my leg or I won't be doing much walking later."

The duke nodded. "Stay away from them," he said in a harsh tone. "If the rumors about them are true, they'll ruin you. They are not a good sort."

Roman frowned. "All right," he said in a quiet tone. He refused to stay away from her, though. Roman couldn't say why, but he knew she was meant to be his. It might be whimsy or he might even be a fool, but he had always followed his instincts. Those very instincts had saved his life. He might be damaged, but he was alive. He couldn't ignore something that had kept him breathing, and he wouldn't let go of a woman that could very well be his future. "I'll heed your advice."

Some things were meant to be. Roman left Thornridge alone and went to his bedchamber to take care of his leg. The duke had followed the same advice from someone else, and that had led him to letting go of Lady Isla. He didn't know how he knew that with certainty, but he did. He would also bet that Thornridge regretted that decision, but would refuse to admit it.

Maybe one day he'd realize that having her was far more important than his pride, but he wouldn't welcome that observation now. Roman would keep those thoughts to himself, at least for now. One day his friend might be open to hearing them, and when that day arrived he'd say his piece.

Three

A thena sighed and strolled into the library the next morning. Their father had been called away on estate business the previous day and she'd been informed there would be a family meeting after breakfast in the library. They all woke at different times and there was no formal breakfast meal. It was easier for them to set a time to meet that would work for the entire family. Athena was a late riser normally, but she had difficulty sleeping the night before. So she'd been awake before Isla, who was usually the first to rise.

She entered the library and found it empty. Surely she wasn't the first to arrive. She had had a tray sent to her room earlier that morning and had only left her chamber a few moments ago. Athena frowned. Where was her family? Had the meeting been cancelled, and no one had bothered to inform her? No, that wasn't possible. They wouldn't have forgotten her.

"You're early," Isla said as she strolled into the library. "I would have thought you'd still be dressing for the day."

Any other day Isla would have been correct. Athena hated mornings. She shrugged. "I woke earlier than normal." That seemed like an understatement; however, she didn't want to explain to her sister why she had trouble sleeping the night before. She'd never told either of her sisters about her encounter by the pond. At first she'd decided against mentioning it to Isla because of how she'd likely react to her riding on the duke's property, and then Maeve had been too engrossed in her latest painting for her to take a break for fear of losing her optimal light.

So she'd kept her own counsel… It was probably for the best. She didn't know exactly how to describe what had happened with Lord Kendal. Honestly, nothing had happened. They talked, and he'd introduced himself, and she'd kept her own name to herself. It was her feelings that confused her. She would wait a while and sort them out before speaking about Lord Kendal. After all, she knew little about the man, and until she gained more insight, her silence was necessary.

"Is something bothering you?" Isla asked.

Her sister was too observant for her own good. Sometimes Athena wished she it was easier to hide things from her oldest sister. "Not at all," she replied in an amiable tone.

Isla stared at her as if she didn't believe her, and why should she? Luckily, she was saved from Isla's interrogation when Maeve and their father entered the library. "Good, you're both here," their father said as a way of greeting Isla and Athena. "Please," he began. "Everyone sit. This won't take long, and then you can go about your day."

They all sat on the settee in the library and their father took the chair to the right of it. They sat in silence and waited for him to speak. "As you all know, Athena and Maeve are set to have their debut ball in a few weeks."

"We do," Athena said. "Has something changed?"

Her father nodded at her. "The debut ball will happen as scheduled," he explained. "It's our travel plans that have to change."

Athena frowned. She did not like the sound of

that. Her time in the country was important to her. If they left London sooner, then she would have less time with Hades. He couldn't come to London with them. "When are we leaving?" she asked.

"In five days," he told her. "It's only a week sooner than planned. I've already informed the servants. Your maids will pack for you in time and be ready to travel with you."

So good of him to inform their servants before them... That was discourteous of her to think, but she couldn't help being displeased. Their father had a large estate to run, and he didn't have to explain himself to any of them.

"Do I have to go?" Isla asked in a petulant tone. She hated society, and for good reason.

"Yes," their father said. "I need you to help oversee the girls' season. I've hired an elderly matron to chaperone, but I expect you to be there with them."

"I understand," Isla replied in a dejected tone. Poor Isla. Her season had been a terrible disappointment. "I'll do as you ask."

"Now that I've explained that there is one other thing we need to discuss," their father said.

They all glanced in his direction. What could there be? Hadn't it been enough to end their quiet days in the country sooner than planned? Yes, Athena wanted a season, but she also wanted the time with Hades she'd been promised.

"I expect you all to be on your best behavior while we are in London." He pinned Athena with a glare as if he was directing this speech at her. "No unlady like behavior." He turned to Maeve. "No staring at people and making them feel uncomfortable." Then he focused his attention on Isla. "And no avoiding company because you find them distasteful." He leaned back in his chair and steepled his fingers together. "We're going to enjoy London. Do you all understand?"

"Yes, father," they chorused together.

Their father was asking a lot of them. Some things were beyond their control. How were they going to enjoy London when society tended to snub them all? She had her doubts any of them would attend the debut ball. She'd voiced that to Maeve and Isla a few weeks ago, and Isla had laughed. Her response was to explain that the ton wouldn't dare not to show their faces. They wouldn't want to offend their father outright and openly. They were more apt to whisper their discord and hope it didn't reach their father's ears.

"Now that we've settled that you are excused. Have a good day."

They all stood and exited the library. Athena was restless once again and decided to take Hades out again. She wouldn't let her hair fly loose this time. That had been silly. Instead, she'd have her made plait it and pinned it up tightly. She wouldn't want any more tangles.

Was it too much to hope that she might cross paths with Lord Kendal again?

ROMAN HAD GONE into town early that morning with Thornridge. Not because he had any interest in going, but because it had seemed like a good idea at the time. He'd regretted it almost immediately. The duke was in a foul mood and grunted more than held a conversation with him.

"What is bothering you?" he asked.

"I'm fine," the duke responded.

Well, that had gotten him nowhere. He could guess, but didn't even know where to begin. He sighed and settled back into the carriage. Perhaps when they returned, he would go for another ride. Perhaps he would find the fiery lady at the pond again. He wanted to know her name. Thornridge hadn't been much help there. He'd not wanted to discuss the neighbor girls or why they were trouble.

"I am thinking I should return home soon," he told the duke. "I wrote my mother finally to inform her I was back in England and I was staying with you. She wasn't too pleased with that information."

"I would think she'd be happy to have you nearby and alive." The duke met his gaze. "But perhaps I am wrong. You were never the favorite son, were you?"

Roman blew out a breath. "I don't think my father believed I was his son." He hadn't ever wanted to admit that aloud. It was the only thing that made sense as to why he'd been treated so horridly as a child. He'd done nothing right. "Though I look more like a James, that didn't matter to him."

"Your father was an arse," Thornridge replied in a cool tone. "Have you asked your mother? Is there a reason he might have believed that?"

He hadn't wanted to broach the topic with his mother. Roman didn't want to offend her, and a small part of him hadn't wanted to know the truth. What if he wasn't his father's son? Then he'd be rolling in his grave at the knowledge that Roman now held the title he'd held so dearly. He might feel like an imposter if he discovered he was not a true heir to the title. What would he do then? "She wouldn't tell me the truth."

"You don't think so?" The duke lifted a brow. "You might be surprised."

"Perhaps," he said in a noncommittal tone. "Either way, it doesn't matter anymore. He's gone, and so is my brother. It may be best to let the past lie where it belongs and move forward."

"Do you really believe that?" his friend asked.

He wanted to. Desperately so... "I have little choice," he answered. "I refuse to live my life with my father's disapproving voice echoing inside my head. I want to be happy."

And perhaps a certain dark-haired beauty was the thing he needed to achieve that elusive emotion. Roman had never been happy. He wasn't sure he would know what that felt like.

Thornridge nodded. "I still think you should speak with your mother about it. I don't believe you will be able to move forward as you wish and find that happiness until you do." He tapped his fingers on the side of the carriage. "When do you think you'll return?"

Roman shrugged. "I haven't made any decisions

yet. Maybe a sennight." He didn't want to leave Thornridge Castle until he learned her name. There were three possibilities, but he wanted the correct one. Should he pay a call on them? No. That would be foolish. He wouldn't know what name to give the servants when he stopped in. Who would he ask to see?

"I think I might come with you," Thornridge told him. "I've stayed longer than I should have."

With that statement, guilt rolled over Roman. "I'm sorry…"

"Don't be," his friend said. "You needed me. I was glad to offer my home to you."

The duke was one of his closest friends. They only had one other friend that was equally as close. Roman hadn't seen him since before he'd left for the war. "How is Pemberton?" he asked. "When was the last time you saw him?"

Thornridge shrugged. "Not since before you arrived. He has changed little."

Viscount Pemberton was one of the biggest scoundrels in the ton. He discarded lovers frequently and was often found in some of the most disreputable gaming hells. Pemberton thought highly of himself and offered no apologies to anyone. He might mutter one begrudgingly to Roman or Thornridge, but only because they were the only two people alive he respected enough to bother. He ha dark blond hair, pale green eyes, and a face that drew more women to him than one man could handle, but the viscount certainly tried.

"I think I'll write to him and tell him I'm returning to London soon. I won't stay with my mother for long. She can be a bit...much." Thornridge had been right in his earlier statement. Cassius had been the favorite of both parents. His mother would welcome him home because she had no choice. He was the earl now, and she depended on him for support.

The duke's lips twitched. "If you're going to visit with Pemberton, keep in mind his proclivities might be more than you wish to participate in."

He laughed. "I am aware of our friend's habits. I think I'll be fine."

Besides, he didn't want to spend his night with any loose women. There was only one woman he wanted in his bed, and he'd gladly marry her to have her there. There were several steps in-between until he had that goal. The first one being discovering her name. Then he'd start courting her in truth.

The carriage rolled to a stop in front of Thornridge Castle. The duke exited, and Roman followed.

"Go inside without me," he told the duke. "I feel the need for a walk." Riding would be too much. His leg was still too stiff after yesterday's jaunt. "My leg needs the exercise after being in the carriage."

Thornridge nodded. "Don't overdo it," he told him. "We will talk more later." He said nothing else. Instead, he turned on his heels and went inside, leaving Roman alone.

Roman took that as his cue to start his walk. He only had one destination in mind, and he hoped he'd find the gorgeous woman he'd met the day before there. Maybe, for once, luck would be in his favor.

Four

R oman strolled into the clearing by the pond at a leisurely pace. Yes, he hoped she would be there, but he also realized rushing would go against his own interests. For several reasons... If he walked too fast, he would aggravate the still healing injuries in his leg, and how would it appear for him to come running up on her? She didn't seem like the typical female and probably wouldn't easily startle; however, she would realize quickly how eager he was to see her again. That would give her an advantage in their exchange, and he wanted to keep them on equal footing. At least for as long as possible...

Everything changed inside of him when he met her. It was almost as if he'd been waiting his entire life to meet her, and now that he had, Roman had one goal. To have her by his side for the rest of their lives. He stopped near a tree and glanced around him, then grinned like the fool he most likely was when he noticed a horse tied to a post in the distance.

He hadn't seen her yet, though. Where had she disappeared to? Roman headed in the direction of the pond, glancing around him as he made his way to where he hoped to find her. Underneath a large tree with leaves budding, he found her on a blanket with a leather-bound book in her lap. She seemed engrossed in the pages and hadn't yet noticed him walking toward her.

Roman stopped in front of her and waited. Slowly, she lifted her head and met his gaze. A smile filled her face as she stared up at him. "You're sneakier than you were last time," she said, then laughed. "Aren't you a surprise?"

He lifted a brow. "Is that so terrible?" Roman didn't wish to tell her about his infirmary yet. The last thing he wanted was for her to see him as some sort of cripple. He had worked hard to overcome his difficulties, and he still had more work to do, but he fully believed he would recover.

She closed the book and tucked it away into a

small bag. He was curious about it, but didn't ask. She stood up and brushed down her trousers. Her hair was bound, and he found he was disappointed that they were not flowing over her as they had been before. Instead, they were wound around her gorgeous face in firmly secured plaits. Finally, she glanced at him and said, "I had hoped to see you again."

"You did?" That surprised him. He hadn't thought she would admit to such a thing. "Why?"

Her smile wasn't bright, but held a bit of sadness. He didn't like it. "Because we won't be here much longer. I wanted to apologize for my rude behavior."

"I didn't think you were rude," he told her as her worlds seared through him. "Where are you going?" He focused on what was most important. Roman couldn't very well court her if he couldn't find her. He had thought he could handle his mother and be seen around London a bit, then return to her. That wouldn't work if she left.

"To London, of course," she said, as if that was the only answer that could be acceptable. "I'm to have my first season." She shrugged. "Well, Maeve and I are."

She was one of the twins... He still didn't know

her name, but at least he could narrow down which one she was not. He smiled. "That's wonderful," he told her. He felt that in his very bones. He had just decided to return home and then go to London. They would be in the same city and he could court her openly during the season.

"It is?" She raised both brows. "I'm afraid I do not understand your happiness at my upcoming season."

He may regret his next words, but he did not see any reason not to tell her. "Because I'm leaving soon too," he explained. "I'll be in London soon enough as well. Perhaps we shall meet again there."

Her smile held more warmth when it slowly filled her face. He basked in it and wanted to lean down and kiss her. I was too soon. Roman didn't wish to frighten her away.

"I would very much like to see you again," she admitted, then tilted her head to the side to study him. "You don't know me. Why do you wish to be around me?"

Did she not realize how truly beautiful she was? There was something absolutely pure about her. When she glanced at him with those inquisitive eyes, he almost became speechless. Somehow, he found enough to utter, "Because you're a surprise I never thought to wish for."

Her eyes widened, and she stepped closer to him. "I feel the same about you," she admitted.

They were so close now he could close the distance and give in to the need to kiss her. He shouldn't. How scandalous would that be? He'd kiss her and compromise her without even knowing her name...

"I should go." His voice came out gruff as he fought his need to kiss her. He would not accost her like a lecherous old man. "You were occupied when I strolled toward you."

"Do you have to leave?" she asked. "I'd like for you to stay."

He could stay and listen to her speak for hours, or not say anything at all. Roman calmed in her presence and just felt content. "Do you think that is wise?"

She studied him for several moments and then said, "If you must leave me, I have one request before you do."

"Anything," he said and meant it.

"Kiss me," she told him.

He couldn't have heard her correctly. "Pardon me?"

She flicked her tongue over her bottom lip and stepped closer. "You heard me, Lord Kendal," she insisted. "Kiss me. I know you want to."

He closed his eyes and groaned. It would be so easy to do as she asked, and he wasn't strong enough to resist her. Now when she was asking him to do the very thing he desperately wanted. Roman cursed and pulled her into his arms, then pressed his lips to hers. His entire body erupted with need at the contact. He slanted his lips over hers and when she opened her mouth on a gasp; he slid his tongue inside her mouth. Their tongues tangled together as their desire became an entity they couldn't control.

Somehow, with great reluctance, Roman stopped. This couldn't happen in a field where anyone could walk up on them. He had to protect her. He took a step back and stared at her, his breathing ragged. "That..."

"Was everything," she finished for him. Her smile was so sensual it gutted him. "Thank you, Lord Kendal. You've told me all I needed to know."

He wished he could think clearly enough to decipher her meaning. "Roman," he told her. "You should definitely call me Roman." He met her gaze. "Tell me your name." He was tired of not knowing that little detail about her. It was important.

"I'm Athena," she told him. "Lady Athena Thompson." She grinned. "I should return home." Athena folded her blanket and placed it in the saddlebag on her horse, along with her small bag with the book. She mounted her horse and then said, "Until we meet again in London, Roman. Don't disappoint me." Then she flicked the reins, and the horse took off. Roman stared after her like a bumbling fool.

"Athena," he whispered her name. "I will see you again." She'd charmed him the first time he'd glanced her way, and now he was most definitely besotted. He couldn't wait to spend more time in her company.

THREE WEEKS LATER...

Athena stared down at the gown she'd had designed for her debut ball. It was a dark green that was too bold for a young debutante about to be presented, but she didn't care. Her hair was piled high on her head, with dark ringlets draping around her face. The pendant with her initial that she'd found with her mother's journal was her only jewelry. The black stone glittered in the candlelight and it almost felt as if her mother stood beside her approvingly.

All she could think about was Roman. He had kissed her. Yes, she had asked him too, but she hadn't thought he actually would. And what a kiss it had been... She touched her lips as if she could feel his lips still there. She would kiss him again. Athena hadn't been certain until that moment, but he was meant to be hers.

That might seem ridiculous to believe, but she did. Athena didn't regret kissing him. It had been a test. At first, it had started out as something she needed, but then it quickly turned into something far more devastating to her. Her heart opened up to him in those fleeting moments, and he had willingly entered. She would bet everything that he had felt what she had. They were drawn to each other for a reason.

A knock echoed through the room, and Isla stepped inside. She wore a gown of deep gold that made her skin glow. Her only jewelry as well was the black stone pendant with her initial. "Are you ready?" Her gown was a declaration in itself. Isla held her head high as she prepared herself to face the ton again. They had flayed her the last time she'd been in London, and she'd fled home to heal.

Athena still didn't know all that had happened to her older sister. She wished she could protect her now from what was to come.

"I am," she told Isla. "Is Maeve done dressing?"

'Almost," Isla said. "There was a slight difficulty with her gown. One of the buttons had loosened, and it had to be repaired. She shouldn't be much longer."

Maeve had decided for a soft peach gown that was more suitable for a debut ball. She was more practical than Athena ever would be. The gown suited her twin, though. They had distinct personalities and their gowns would show the world who they were. Soon enough they would be out in society and they would be subject to the same ridicule that still haunted Isla. Were they fools to go through that same torturous gossip and disdain from the ton?

"Let's go down into the hall then and wait for her. We should enter the ballroom together." They should present a united front to the buzzards. They might not want to pick over their remains if they couldn't actually reach them. She looped her arm through Isla's. "We will be with you every step of the way."

Isla sucked in a deep breath. "Thank you," she said in a quiet tone. "I'll be all right. I promise."

She thought she heard her mutter something under her breath. Had Isla said, at least he will not be here. Did she mean the Duke of Thornridge? That was the only he that Isla avoided. What had happened between them? All Athena knew with certainty was that the duke had broken her sister's heart, and both of them seemed miserable. The duke, the last time Athena had seen him, had been as forlorn as Isla. Maybe one day they would find their way back to each other. It was clear to her they were unhappy apart, so they might erase that unwelcome emotion if they admitted they belonged together. She didn't know if that was possible, or if they would be open to it, but the solution was there for them to grasp on to.

They were not in the hall long before Maeve joined them. Her hair was secured in an elegant chignon, but she did not have as many loose curls as Athena did. She also had on the pendant with her initial. They all had chosen to honor their mother, and Athena prayed they would not regret that choice. The peach gown enhanced Maeve's beauty. "You look beautiful," she told her twin.

"Thank you," Maeve said, then smiled. "You do as well."

"It's time," Isla told them both, then braced her

shoulders. She was preparing for something unpleasant and it hurt Athena that her sister felt that need. "Let's descend the stairs and let them announce us. My maid told me that it is a crush. Everyone who is anyone is here."

That should make Athena happy, but dread filled her. Something terrible was about to happen. She only prayed it didn't leave emotional scars as it had with Isla, or worse. "We can do this," she said, more for herself than her sisters, but it applied to them all. Slowly, they descended the stairs, and with each step, they accepted their destiny. They would make it to the end. Nothing could destroy them if they didn't allow it.

Five

Roman wished he could have skipped visiting his mother and gone straight to London. Her ramblings and reprimands had both been tedious and frustrating. She had seemed happy to see him, but he didn't think it was for his sake. His mother was practical and knew having one of her sons still alive was to her benefit. If one of his cousins inherited the title, she might not be so well off. As the mother of the earl, she was held in much higher regard in society. The Dowager Countess of Kendal enjoyed having the ear of the most prominent members of society and wanted to stay exactly where she'd been placed upon her husband's death. She didn't have to be a wife, but had all the benefits that allowed it.

It had been an exercise in futility. He listened to her berate him for his absence while in the same breath, asking when he would leave again. She also intended to go to London for the season and hoped she would see him there. Roman didn't actually believe she wanted him to have attend anything regarding the season, but she probably did hope he would marry and secure an heir for the earldom. Not because she had any hope of having grandchildren, but because she would so hate to fall into a state of destitution, or something she'd consider akin to beggary.

He was happy to be away from her loving company. It had left him feeling cold, and he had a deep need for warmth again. Which was why he found himself at the townhouse of the Earl of Harwood's London townhouse. There were so many people there to attend the debut ball for the twins. He had to wonder if all of the guests actually received an invitation. No one seemed to have been turned away, that was certain. It surprised Roman to find that he had an invitation. Had Athena ensured he would have one? When had the invitations actually been sent?

Roman wanted to believe she wished for him to attend. He wanted to see her again. It had been a very long while since he had seen her. All right it had been a little more than a fortnight, but it seemed far longer. He glanced toward the two gentlemen who had agreed to attend with him. "Are you prepared for this?" The carriage almost seemed too small for all three of them. None of them were small in stature.

They were all eligible to the ladies searching for a husband, but Thornridge would have the biggest draw. He pinned Roman with a glare. "I would rather go with Pemberton to one of his favorite brothels."

"So would I," the viscount added in a jovial tone. "I can definitely suggest a few more pleasurable choices. Why are we here again?"

"To watch Kendal act the fool," Thornridge drawled. "I told him he should stay away from this family, but he's determined to ruin himself with this pursuit."

"The chit cannot be as terrible as you're suggesting," Pemberton said. "I heard they're all beauties."

Thornridge was silent for a few moments, then said in a tone so quiet Roman almost missed what he'd said, "No one lady is more beautiful than Isla." He cleared his throat. "They're all beautiful. That is their allure, but you will regret being in their company."

Roman wanted to ask questions, but he held them back. He didn't think Thornridge would discuss what had happened. He clearly had feelings for Athena's sister, but he didn't know how deep they went. Had Isla broken his heart or was it much worse than that... Had Thornridge been his own undoing and ensured he would forever have a hole in his life because he'd done what he should instead of what he desired. Roman would not follow that path. He'd been the dutiful son and went down the expected path already. That had not gotten him anything but pain. He wanted happiness, and that meant claiming the only woman he had ever wanted in his life.

"You're wrong," Roman said. "Some things are worth every risk. She is important to me. If that is too much for you, then perhaps you and Pemberton should go to a brothel and leave me here."

The duke shook his head. "This is where we will be. You may need us."

"Then keep your opinions to yourself. Some things shouldn't be spoken." Roman frowned. "And do try to enjoy yourself. It is a ball. They're meant for entertainment."

"Blasphemy," Pemberton mumbled. "Societal events are never as entertaining as the wicked variety." His green eyes twinkled with mischief. "Though I suppose with the right lady, a ball could be more wicked than even the most decadent house of sin. I'll see what I can manage at this one."

Roman closed his eyes and prayed. Pemberton would do whatever he pleased. He always did. "Do try to be discreet," he told the viscount.

"I'm always the very picture of discretion," Pemberton scoffed. "Ladies love me. They cannot help themselves."

"You should," Thornridge said. "I do not understand how you have not been trapped into marriage yet."

"Because of that very discretion I mentioned before," Pemberton said. "That and I do not bed innocents. That's a sure way to end up with a knot tying me to one woman for the rest of my days." He shuddered. "That's a fate I'd like to avoid for as long as possible."

The carriage came to a stop at the entrance finally. It felt as if they had been in the carriage forever. They each stepped out of the carriage and headed up the steps leading to the townhouse. It didn't take that long to reach the ballroom. They were each announced, but no one truly paid any attention. At least not that he noticed... There were far too many guests attending for anyone to be observant of the room as a whole.

Roman wanted to see one woman. He tried to find her but was failing.

"Is this the ball of the season?" Pemberton asked. "I didn't know the debut of two young ladies would be such a draw."

"It's not simply two young ladies," Thornridge said. "It's these specific young ladies, and who the identity of their mother or more specifically the family she derived from."

"What do you mean?" Roman frowned. Thornridge had not been forthcoming with information. He had just warned him to stay away, but gave no real reason for the censure. "What family?

The duke opened his mouth, but then closed it and shook his head. It seemed as if Roman would not get the answers he craved. "Have it your way," Roman told him. "I'll find out either way."

He left Thornridge and Pemberton together and went in search of the woman he'd come to the ball for, and it didn't take too long for him to find her.

She was on the edge of the ballroom, surrounded by gentlemen. Her dark green dress was exquisite and made her a beacon in a sea of dresses. Roman moved toward her and when he reached the circle surrounding her, she glanced up. Her smile when she met his gaze sent warmth through him. This is what he'd been missing. Her.

Roman held out his hand. "Dance with me," he said. It should have been a question, but he it hadn't come out that way. He should have asked to see her dance card. What if someone else was supposed to lead her on to the floor?

She grinned and placed her hand in his. "I was saving this one just for you."

He didn't know if that was true, and he didn't much care. He led her to the floor and almost laughed when he realized what music was being played. It was a waltz. Thank God. Something was finally going right in his life.

Roman ignored the pain in his leg. It was worth it to have her in his arms. She fit in his arms as if she was made for him alone. "You're beautiful," he told her. "I missed you."

Perhaps he was saying all the wrong things. He shouldn't rush forward as if she was already his, even though in his mind she had always belonged to him. She had a choice, and he had to respect it.

"I missed you too," she said. "I'm glad you're here."

She was perfect, and to him, she always would be. His future lay with her. He twirled her around the floor, and as the strands of the waltz floated over them, everyone else disappeared. For those moments, it seemed as if the world disappeared and left them alone, with nothing standing in their way. "Can I call on you?"

"Always," she answered immediately. "You should meet my sisters."

He wanted to. Roman wanted to know everything about her. "I'm sure they're as lovely as you are."

Athena grinned, and that dimple in her left cheek drew his eyes. He wanted to kiss her there, and then give all of his attention to her lips. Later, once she agreed to be his wife, he'd kiss far more than that. Roman wanted to taste every inch of her and love her completely. He could wait, but he hoped he wouldn't have to keep his desires restrained for too long.

"Well," she began. "My twin does mostly look

like me. I would understand if you think she's as beautiful as I am."

He frowned. "How can your twin not look completely like you?" Roman would know Athena anywhere. He hadn't even noticed another woman that might resemble her and could not imagine two of her.

"Our dimples are the only difference," she admitted. "If you're ever uncertain, our smiles will tell the truth every time."

"Your dimple." He glanced at her left cheek. "Is adorable. How is hers not like yours?"

"It's on her right cheek," Athena explained, then shrugged one shoulder as he led her around the floor. He didn't know how she had managed that. "It's like looking into my own reflection. A quirk of nature, I suppose."

He nodded. "I'll keep that in mind." Roman wanted to be alone with her. Even if it is only for a few moments. "Can we leave the ballroom?" Roman didn't know where to take her, as he wasn't familiar with the townhouse. He'd never been to the Earl of Harwood's residence. He'd been at war, and then convalescing for over a year. Roman hadn't had time to socialize.

"I would love that," Athena said, then glanced

around the room. "Lead me over to the other side of the room. As the music ends, we can sneak out by the balcony doors. The garden has a maze in it. I'd love to show you."

Roman did as she suggested and then not long after that, they were outside on the balcony. There were several guests outside enjoying the cooler air the night sky offered. It had been quite hot inside the ballroom. She led him to a nearby stairway, and they headed down.

"How far is this maze?" he asked.

"Not much farther," she told him.

They were passing by a rosebush with buds just starting to form. He wished they had already been in bloom. Roman had the urge to pluck one and present it to her. He would give her dozens of roses later. They reached the edge of the maze. "It's not elaborate," she explained. "But it is tricky if you're not familiar with it."

"Lead the way," he told her. "They were completely alone now, and they didn't need to enter the maze, but he wanted to ensure they wouldn't be interrupted."

He walked with her through the pathways until they reached the center. There was a fountain in the center. A simple one that trickled water from its spout surrounded by vines and flowers. "My mother had this made." She glanced at him. "My father said it was her wishing fountain. That if one hoped to hold on to love, they could throw something inside that has meaning to them and their wish would be granted." She turned toward the fountain. "It's silly and a lot of the ton would think it is witchcraft if it did work. Then we would truly be shunned."

Roman lifted his hand and placed his fingers on her chin, then lifted it so she would meet his gaze. "I don't need to make a wish for love," he told her. "And if anyone believes ill of you, then I'll ensure they never make you feel less than the wonderful woman you are."

"You're sweet," she said, and stepped out of his reach. "But you cannot control the ton. They'll never truly accept us."

"Does this have to do with your mother?" Thornridge had mentioned something earlier and he had to know the truth. He couldn't fight a battle without all the information. "Tell me about her."

Athena sighed. "I never knew her. She died when I was born." Athena turned away from him. "The rumors are that she was a witch. One of her ancestors had been accused of it in Salem, Massachusetts in the seventeenth century," she began. "He was acquitted, but the stigma stayed. It followed her from America back to England when she married my father."

He nodded. "And no one wants that to follow into their families. Then why is everyone here for your debut? What do they expect will happen?"

"They expect we'll fail," she said. "And they want to witness every agonizing moment of it. Isla fell in love during her first season, and he ended up spurning her. I don't know if I would survive a broken heart."

"That will not happen." Thornridge had made a mistake. He knew with certainty then that the duke had been the one to destroy the woman he loved. Why had he done it? That didn't matter in the end, though. Roman would not follow that same path. "You're my everything. Surely you understand that. I could no more stay away from you than I could quit breathing. You're my sunshine and without you, the world is a dark place. I need your warmth."

She inhaled sharply. "Don't disappoint me. Words can be easily spoken, but in the end they don't always equate to actions."

"You'll see," he promised. "I didn't survive a war only to lose in the end." Roman took a step toward her. She turned toward him and then with one more step, she was in his arms, then his lips were on hers. The kiss was more than a promise, it was a declaration. He would marry her. Even if he had to kidnap her and ride as fast as possible to Scotland to prove it to her. They belonged together.

Six

S unlight bathed over Athena as she strolled with her sisters in Hyde Park. They had decided to partake in the afternoon promenade with the rest of the ton. Not that Isla had been enthusiastic about their decision to take a walk in the park. Isla wanted nothing more than to hide in their townhouse or, better yet, return to their father's country house. Athena couldn't really blame her older sister for her desire to remain outside of society. None of them had been welcoming. They were invited to social events, but they were not truly welcome there. The matrons of society had no real reason to exclude them. They were all waiting for that reason to be forthcoming and make the Thompson girls' pariahs.

Athena would not be the one to give them that reason...

She doubted Maeve would, either. Isla kept herself separate from everybody on purpose. She hoped that no one actually noticed her long enough to find anything troubling about her. There was no scandal to be found if she didn't actually speak or do much more than hug a wall at every social event they attended. They all did everything they could to not only appear respectable, but their very actions were beyond reproachable.

None of that aided in what they needed most...

Rumors were still spreading faster than they could ever be squelched. Their very presence instigated them from forming and as long as they remained in London, they would continue to grow. The latest whispers to reach their ears had been about the Earl of Kendal and how Athena had somehow woven some wickedness to lure his attentions.

Athena had, of course, done nothing of the kind.

She couldn't, and wouldn't, explain any of that. No one would listen or believe her if she did. Her real dilemma concerned the earl himself. Athena didn't want his reputation harmed because the ton refused to believe her to be respectable. She was starting to understand Isla's reluctance to attend the season. The earl had come to mean a great deal to Athena in a short time. Her heart ached at the thought of never seeing him again.

"Lady Athena," a woman said. "How lovely to cross paths with you and your sisters."

Athena glanced up and met the gaze of Lady Atherton. Her daughter had her debut this season as well and she did not like that Athena and Maeve had caught the attention of some of the most eligible gentlemen looking for a wife. "The pleasure is ours," Athena said, then pasted a smile on her face that she didn't feel. The viscountess demonstrated an unpleasantness with every word and deed she presented to the world. What did she hope to gain by approaching them?

Maeve froze next to Athena, and Isla held her breath. Her sisters knew something awful was about to descend upon them. They would not like whatever Lady Atherton had planned... Athena held herself still and waited.

"You're familiar with my daughter, Miss Bethany Smythe?" Lady Atherton gestured toward the woman at her side. "She had her debut the week before yours." Why was she addressing Athena and practically ignoring her sisters?

"We've been introduced," she replied carefully. Athena nodded toward Miss Bethany. "It's good to see you again. I trust you're well."

Miss Bethany smiled. "I am Lady Athena. It's a lovely day, is it not?" The viscountess' daughter was a shy girl and doomed to become a wallflower. Athena actually liked her. She was nothing like her mother.

"Indeed, it is," Athena agreed and returned her warm smile with one of her own. "Are you attending the Covington musicale tonight?" Isla had complained about going to it earlier, but Maeve had been the one that wished to attend. Maeve was the more artistic of the three of them and the only one that had any musical talent. She favored the pianoforte, but they heard the Covingtons were proficient in string instruments. It might be entertaining. She prayed they wouldn't leave with an earache of some sort.

"Is it true what we've heard," Lady Atherton asked, ignoring Athena's question about the Covington musicale.

"I couldn't possibly say," Athena answered. "As I have no way of discerning what you heard to confirm any truthfulness of it." She barely refrained from rolling her eyes. What Lady Atherton had overheard or whatever gossip she had readily gathered was most likely inaccurate. But Athena could only guess at the contents of the falsehood, and she really didn't wish to add any additional fodder for them to pick over.

"Then you haven't heard?" Lady Atherton practically gleamed, and not in a good way. She was like a scavenger bird about to pick their bones clean with glee. "It concerns your earl."

Maeve moved closer to Athena, but didn't say a word. It was her show of support for what was to come. Isla became stiff next to her. She'd had her own problems with society and it appeared as if Athena was about to experience a bit of her own unpleasantness. "I'm afraid I don't understand your meaning. What earl do you refer to?" She refused to give the viscountess any satisfaction in admitting her connection to the Earl of Kendal. Roman was indeed her earl. He'd all but declared himself already. That woman didn't need to know any of that, though.

"You can act innocent, but we know the truth." Lady Atherton leaned in closer. "Everyone is talking about it. You charmed him into submission already, and a betrothal is imminent." Lady Atherton winked. "The only thing everyone is uncertain about is if you seduced him already or not." She waved her hand dismissively. "Though does that truly matter? He is yours now, and no one will be able to steal his attention from you. That is the magic of your family line, is it not?"

How dare he... "There is one thing you're correct about Lady Atherton. Everyone talks, and no one takes the time to wonder if what they speak about should be. Good day." With those words, she spun on her heels and headed out of Hyde Park. She didn't stop to wonder if her sisters followed. It was unnecessary to do so. They would never abandon her.

One thing was obvious. She couldn't stay in London. Isla had been right. They were not worth her time, and she had to protect Lord Kendal. He deserved better than to have his name attached to hers. She would beg her father to allow her to return home. Her horse was there, and that was enough comfort for her. The season and the ton had lost all of its appeal to her.

ROMAN MISSED ATHENA. He had hoped to pay a call on her the day before, but his mother had decided to come to London. She'd decided it was time for him to marry and he couldn't possibly choose a wife without her assistance. He didn't have the heart to tell her he'd already met the woman he hoped would become his wife. If he had, she might have insisted on meeting her and the last thing he needed was for his mother to frighten Athena away before he had a chance to win her hand.

He liked his chance of her already agreeing, but he didn't want to assume she'd say yes. A woman deserved to be wooed and he would continue to court her. Roman whistled as he walked to the entrance of the Earl of Harwood's townhouse. He lifted the knocker on the door and rapped it twice, then waited. The door opened and a tall man with salt and pepper hair greeted him. "May I help you?"

"I'm here to call on Lady Athena," he told the man and handed him his card. "Is she receiving?"

The man stared at the card and frowned. "Please come in." Roman entered and stood inside the foyer waiting for the man to tell him where to go and wait for Athena. The man continued to frown at his card. "Give me a moment." The man didn't wait for Roman to agree. He bustled out of the room and left Roman in the foyer alone. How odd. Was he uncertain if Athena was available?

A few moments later, steps from the hallway

caught his attention. He smiled and then frowned. He had thought it was Athena, but instead her twin headed toward him. "Lord Kendal," she greeted him. "Please come into the sitting room with me. I've ordered refreshments. You''ll have tea with us, yes?"

"Of course," he said. Roman hadn't thought he'd be left alone with Athena. There had to be a chaperone of some sort, but he had a bad feeling in his stomach. Why had she not come to escort him into the sitting room? What was Maeve not saying?

They entered the sitting room, and their other sister, Isla, waited inside. She sat on a settee with a book in her lap. She glanced up when they entered, and frowned. Isla stood and greeted them. "Lord Kendal," she said in a surprised tone. "How good to see you."

Where was Athena? He smiled. "I trust I have not come at an inopportune time."

She glanced down at her book. "Not at all." Isla set it on a table and glanced at Maeve.

"I ordered tea and biscuits sent in." She gestured toward a nearby chair. "Please have a seat, Lord Kendal."

Isla and Maeve sat on the settee and stared at him expectantly. He didn't know what to say. Roman wanted to demand they fetch Athena. She was the reason he'd come to visit. He cleared his throat. "What social engagement are you attending this evening?" He wanted to ensure he saw Athena later and hopefully dance with her again.

"We are staying in tonight," Isla said. "It's been a trying couple of days."

What had happened? "Has it?" He lifted a brow. "I trust it hasn't been too difficult." Roman wanted to glance toward the door, but somehow refrained from doing so.

Maeve fidgeted in her seat, and Isla twisted her hands together in her lap. Neither of them met his gaze. Finally, Maeve glanced up. "I understand you have come to pay a call on Athena."

"I have," he agreed. "Is she delayed?"

"It's not that simple," Isla said, then sighed.

He was about to ask her to clarify when a maid walked in with a tea tray and set it on a nearby table. "Do you wish me to pour?" the maid asked.

"No," Isla told her. "We will take care of it. Thank you, Sarah."

The maid curtsied and then left the room. Isla turned her attention to him. "Tea, my lord?"

Isla stood and poured tea into the cups and handed one to him, then Maeve, and took her own back to the settee. He sipped the tea, but he didn't actually want it. Roman frowned and waited. Surely they would explain where Athena was now.

Maeve blew out a breath, then set her teacup down on the table. "As we were saying..." She frowned. "We know you wish to see Athena, but she's not here."

"She's not?" Why didn't they say that already? What did he fail to understand? The butler could have told him that at the door. Why did they invite him in and make him wait to impart that news?

Isla shook her head. "She has returned home. To the country."

He felt as if someone had punched him in the gut. "I don't understand." They had a good night. He'd kissed her. Roman wanted to kiss her again, and soon.

"It's hard to explain," Maeve began. "Suffice to say the ton isn't welcoming. They make us all feel... inferior, and Athena decided to end her season early."

What the bloody hell had happened? "I see..." Roman didn't quite understand, but he could guess. He had heard some of the rumors. He would have to go to Athena. There was only one solution to this dilemma. She thought it best to withdraw from society, from their budding relationship. Roman didn't accept that. He set his teacup down. "If you'll pardon me." He stood. "I must leave now. Thank you for your hospitality."

"You're going after her, aren't you?" Isla asked as he reached the door.

He turned and smiled. "Of course I am." There was no other answer to give her.

"Good," she said and gave him a sad smile. "At least some men are brave enough to claim love when it is freely given."

Roman sighed. His friend had made a grave error when he had set aside his own feelings. One day he'd tell the duke how much of a fool he had been, and if Thornridge was lucky, he wouldn't be too late to claim the woman that held his heart.

"Have faith," he told Isla. "One day, he might surprise you."

"It's too late for that," she said. "Go. Athena needs you."

Roman nodded and left the townhouse. He had a trip to plan for, and the love of his life to find.

Seven

A thena set her reticule on her bed, then flopped down next to it and sighed. It had been a long journey home, but she had finally arrived. Her reticule held the pendant from her mother's box inside of it, and she hadn't wanted to lose it. She should put it away to ensure that would never happen. It would be all right in her reticule a little while longer. Where would it disappear to in her own bedchamber?

She pulled the bell by her bed to summon her maid. Now that she was home, she wanted to go see her horse and then take a swift, exhilarating ride. It had taken her three extra days to make it back to the country estate. Her father had insisted that they travel at a more sedate pace, and the coachman hadn't wanted to upset the Earl of Harwood. So he had followed her father's instructions to the letter. They had stopped overnight at three inns on the journey home. If the coachman had listened to her and changed horses at each inn instead, she would have been home much sooner.

Her maid came into the bedchamber. "You need me, my lady?"

"Yes," Athena said. "Help me out of this gown. I'm going for a ride." She didn't need assistance in to the trousers she used for riding, but the gown and her corset was impossible to remove on her own. Men's clothing was so much easier to manage. A lady had too many laces and buttons to do them all on her own.

It didn't take long for her maid to undo the buttons on the back of her dress. Athena stepped out of it and her maid hung it on a nearby hook to be cleaned and pressed later. "Do you wish to remove your stays as well?"

"I do," Athena answered. "They are too constricting to ride in." Isla had chastised her for removing them, but her older sister didn't understand. Athena liked to breathe while she was racing through the fields. The last thing she needed was to faint while her horse galloped along. She'd be dead for sure once she fell off and broke her neck.

Her maid loosened the laces on her corset. Athena sighed as she pulled it off and set it on her bed. It was always a relief when she was able to remove her corset. She went over to her armoire and found her riding clothes, then quickly dressed. She sat on her bed and pulled on her riding boots. Another item that was usually reserved for men and she'd had made specially for her. Luckily, none of the shops in town wanted to offend her father and had reluctantly agreed to make the items for her. Though the bootmaker was easier than the tailor to convince. They were not as good as Hessians, but she didn't care. They were not something she wore out in society. All Athena needed was something comfortable and durable.

"I don't know how long I'll be," she told her maid. "I'll ring for you when I'm back in my chamber if I need your assistance."

"Very well, my lady," she replied, then curtsied. "I'll unpack your trunks and have everything organized for you."

"Thank you," Athena replied. She smiled. "It's so good to be home."

That smile remained on her face all the way to the stables until she reached Hades' stall. Her horse made a loud whinny when she stroked his mane. "Did you miss me" She held out some sugar cubes for him and he licked them off her hand. "I definitely missed you. Let's go for a ride."

Athena gestured toward a stable hand to help her. She prepared Hades herself as much as possible. Once the saddle was secured, she led Hades over to a mounting block. She could climb on without one, but she preferred the extra help when it was available. Her bag of snacks, along with her mother's journal, was already in her saddlebag. She had made a lot of progress since she'd first started reading it. There wasn't much left of the journal and she would have to pass it on to Maeve. Isla wanted to be the last to read it.

She kept Hades at a sedate walk until they were some distance from the house. Then she pressed her knee into his side to tell him she wanted to go faster. Hades took off and raced across the field. Athena leaned down and enjoyed the wind whipping across her face. There was no better feeling than riding her horse as fast as she could. She pulled back on the reins. It was time to slow down. They had already gone farther than usual. The pond she normally stopped at passed by in a whirlwind. Perhaps she should circle back...

Hades buckled when he stepped into a hole, and she went flying off his back. Athena landed on the ground hard, but fortunately, they had already slowed. Her pride was more bruised than anything. She started to pull herself up and winced. Her hip burned with pain and it hurt to move.

Hoofbeats pounded on the ground. It wasn't Hades. Her horse, thank heavens, hadn't been injured either. He trotted next to her and whinnied. Athena glanced around her and that's when she noticed him. Another rider was barreling towards them at a breakneck speed. He slowed down as he reached her. "Are you all right?" he asked.

She frowned. "Why are you here?" The Earl of Kendal, Roman, had come for her. Athena was certain of it.

"You didn't answer me," he responded. "Did you hurt yourself?" Roman slid off of his horse and walked toward her.

"I'm perfectly all right," she said and jutted her chin upward. "Now you can leave."

He laughed. "Darling, I'm not going anywhere without you."

In response, the sky opened up and started to pour rain over them. She glanced up and cursed the unfortunate weather. She was drenched through. "We need to get out of this rain." She couldn't walk far, and incidentally, they wouldn't have to. "Follow me. There's an old hunting cabin not far."

They would have their confrontation in something resembling shelter, at least...

ROMAN HELD the reins of his horse and followed her as she led her own horse to wherever the hunting cabin was located. He didn't know the area well enough to be certain there was actually a cabin nearby. Though he didn't think she would have any reason to lie to him.

Finally, they reached a building. Not that he would call it much of a hunting cabin. When was the last time anyone had come out here? It was not in shambles exactly, but it was definitely abandoned. "Why is this no longer in use?" he asked.

She shrugged as she tied her horse to a nearby post. "This belongs to the Duke of Thornridge. You would have to ask him." He did the same and then they went inside. It was dusty, but it still had all of its furnishings. He went over to the hearth and luckily there was kindling nearby that they could use for a fire. Roman arranged them and quickly lit a fire. It took a while for it to grow enough to provide warmth, but he was satisfied with his work.

He turned toward her. "Now tell me how badly you were injured?"

"I told you I am all right," she insisted. "My side will have a bruise, but it'll heal. Nothing to concern yourself with."

Roman sighed. She was so damned headstrong, but he liked that about her. "I won't ask again then." He stared at her. "There are other things that are far more important we need to discuss."

She lifted a brow. Her ice-blue eyes held curiosity and something else he couldn't quite identify. "I am glad you have your priorities, my lord."

He shook his head and sighed. "We're back to formalities, are we?" Roman moved over to her side. "I thought we had progressed past all of that."

"We had," she said. "But that was a mistake."

"We are not moving backwards," he said in a firm tone. "Your sisters were not forthcoming, but I can guess what the issue is. I won't let you run away and hide."

"What do you think you know?" She had that defiance in her tone that he almost admired, if it wasn't being used against him. "We've barely had any time together. It's been nothing but slips of time that can be easily set aside. You're better off not having me in your life."

"I don't agree," he said. Roman had known the moment he met her she was the woman for him. He had also known that she might require convincing of that fact. "The only thing I'll ever regret is walking away from you. Nothing in life is easy, and sometimes the things that are the hardest are the most worthwhile. I've seen a lot of atrocities, but you're not one of them." He lifted his hand and cupped her cheek in his hand. "You love, are the one thing I have always wished for and never imagined I could have. I'll never be able to let that go. Don't ask me to."

She closed her eyes. "My family..."

"Is not the reason I started courting you." He smiled. "I know what they say about your mother." Roman pulled her into his arms. "Let me be clear. Even if that nonsense was true, I would not care. I would want you despite it, or maybe because of it. Either way, I don't give a damn. The ton can go to hell for all I care. You're the one thing I cannot live without. Do you understand?"

Athena sighed. "You might come to regret that."

"No, love," he told her. "I won't ever regret you. I promise you that. The only things that are ever worth regretting are the things we do not do, and loving you had made me happy."

Roman's heart raced inside his chest. He had to make her believe that he couldn't live without her. This all had happened so fast, but all he could do was be honest with her. In a more perfect world, they would have time to sort it all out. If the ton were not full of bigoted fools, she wouldn't have run home. But none of that mattered in the end. As long as they were together, they could find their way through anything.

"You make me happy too," she admitted. Athena licked her lips. "Kiss me.

"There's nothing I'd like more," he said. Roman had dreamed about kissing her every night since the first time his lips had touched hers. He wanted too much more with her, but this might not be the time for that.

He pulled her flush against his body and kissed her deeply. She sighed, and he slipped his tongue inside her mouth. Her clothes were soaked, but then again, so was his. He could kiss her forever and it wouldn't be nearly long enough. Roman had to stop, though. "If we stay in these wet clothes, we might catch our death."

Athena's lips twitched. "Why, my lord, are you trying to seduce me?"

"I..." Roman was speechless. "No... I mean..."

She winked and then pulled her shirt free from her breeches. The white fabric was so wet it was nearly transparent. Her chemise underneath was the only reason he couldn't see her plump breasts, but that wasn't much of a barrier, either. Athena yanked her shirt over her head and undid the strings of her breeches. She pulled off her boots and let her breeches fall to the ground. "Don't worry, love." She stood before him in nothing but her chemise. "I want you to seduce me. Now it's your turn. Take off those wet clothes and come keep me warm. I don't know that we have any blankets to help with that endeavor."

Sweet torture. She was so damned perfect. Roman had never stripped so fast in his entire life. Once he stood before her in nothing but his smalls he stepped toward her. She wrapped her arms around his neck, and he lowered his head to kiss her. He slid her chemise up and caressed her stomach and hips, then slid his hand up until he could cup her breast in the palm of his hand. She moaned as he tweaked a nipple between his thumb and finger.

"Are you certain," he asked as he trailed kisses over her neck. He didn't want to take advantage of her, but she was so damn sweet and irresistible.

"You said we only regret the things we don't do," she said. "I don't want to have any regrets. Make me yours."

Roman groaned and pulled her chemise off and led her over to a settee. It had seen better days, but it still looked comfortable, just worn. He lowered her on to it and then leaned down to press his lips to hers, then he moved down and licked a nipple. She moaned. He wanted to taste her everywhere. This would be her first time, and he wanted it to be good for her.

"I love you," he said. Then he licked her other breast. Roman cupped her between her thighs and slid a finger through her folds.

"That feels…" She moaned as he rubbed her clit. "Roman, yes, do that again."

He smiled and decided to taste her sweetness. Roman wanted to hear her scream his name as he licked her into her climax. He spread her thighs and kissed her sensitive nub. She began to writhe beneath him. Athena's breathing became ragged. He slid a finger into her core as he sucked her sensitive nub into his mouth. "Roman," she screamed as her body shook. "I've never..."

"You are perfect," he said as he slid his smalls off. He had to be inside her.

"I'm not," she said. "But I'm glad you think so."

Roman joined her on the settee and started to kiss her again. "This might be uncomfortable. At least the first time."

She nodded. "I know. I don't want to stop."

Thank heaven... He settled between her things and began to push inside of her. Roman kissed her as he slid slowly inside her heat. He had to make her feel good, but he couldn't be certain she would enjoy this part, at least not the first time. Finally, he was all the way in. He gritted his teeth and stilled.

"That wasn't so bad," she said. "Is that all?"

He laughed. "No, love," he said and pulled back out and then slid in again.

"Oh..." She moaned. "Yes. Do that again."

She was so demanding, and he loved it. Roman thrust into her again and again until she writhed beneath him again. He was so close to his own climax, but he wanted her to find her release again. He wanted to feel her squeezing him as he came.

Roman reached beneath them and rubbed her clit as he thrust inside of her. She moaned and shattered, and he quickly followed.

Everything went black as his own release spread through him. He'd been with other women, but it had never been like that. He rolled to his side and pulled her with him. "Marry me," he said. He should have asked her before he'd taken her virginity, but he hadn't been thinking clearly.

"I thought that was a given," she said, then chuckled. "I love you, Roman. Of course, I'll marry you."

"Good," he said. "Otherwise, I would be kidnapping you and we would make a mad dash to Scotland."

She laughed. "I don't believe an elopement of that magnitude will be necessary. Though you will have to speak with my father. I do want his permission, but I will add that on the chance he says no that mad dash would be acceptable to me"

"I will speak with him immediately. Though not until after this storm passes. It doesn't appear to be letting up. We might be trapped in this cabin overnight."

Athena pressed her lips to his then settled back into his arms. "I'm all right with that. There are far worse things than sleeping in your arms. It truly is one of life's greatest pleasures. At least in my opinion..."

"Mine as well," he agreed. "Rest, love. I'll keep you safe." He closed his eyes and fell asleep with her in his arms. Life was good. Nothing could go wrong as long as he had Athena.

Eight

A chill slid up Athena's spine, and she groaned. The warm blanket that had kept her cozy had suddenly disappeared. She flicked her eyelids open and frowned. Where was she? She stretched and then groaned again, this time in pain. It was then she remembered everything. Including the fall from Hades and the reason her hip bit with a harsh ache that hadn't improved overnight.

"You have a fine bruise on your hip," Roman said. "We should have taken that into consideration. I'm an arse for taking advantage of you when you are injured."

She stared up at him. "I'm perfectly fine," Athena told him. "It's a minor injury, and you did nothing I didn't want you to do. So stop feeling guilty." She sat up. "How long have you been awake?"

"Not long," he said. "I went to check on the horses. The sun should be up soon, and it would be prudent to ride back as soon as it does."

She smiled. Roman had dressed, but she still sat there without a stitch on, and for some reason that didn't bother her at all. If she wanted to, she was certain she could charm him out of his clothes. Especially since his gaze kept trailing over her bare flesh and he paid particular attention to her chest. He liked her breasts, and she wasn't above using that to her advantage. "Are you certain I should put my clothes back on?" Athena trailed her fingers over the side of one of her breasts.

He swallowed hard. "As much as I'd like to keep you just as you are," Roman began. "I'm afraid you'll get cold soon enough. The fire in the hearth has died down and I don't wish to start another when we need to leave shortly."

Athena sighed. "I do admit that a chill roused me from sleep. I suppose I should dress." She stood up and stretched. Her hip ached, but stretching helped ease it a bit. She reached for her chemise and pulled it over her head and then retrieved the rest of her clothes and dressed quickly.

Roman sighed. "You shouldn't be able to wear men's breeches, love. You're a temptation in a gown, but your derriere is pure decadence in a gentleman's trousers."

"You will not convince me that it is in my best interest not to don them while I ride. I've had this argument with my father, and I will not have it with you." Athena glared at him. "I don't wear them outside of our property. I'll never wear them riding in Hyde Park." She rolled her eyes. "I do understand some decorum is necessary. But when I ride Hades, I like the freedom breeches allow."

"I had no intention of ordering you out of them." Roman's gaze trailed over her body. "At least not in the way you're suggesting."

She laughed. "Darling, you just had a sound argument as to why I needed to put my clothes back on. Do not tell me that you now have reconsidered." Athena adored this man...

"I much prefer you in a state of undress," he agreed. "But we do not have time to frolic any longer. The sun is rising, and I need to see you home." Roman tilted his head to the side. "Is your father in residence?"

Her father had sent her home with servants. He wouldn't be there waiting for them. For that, she was grateful, since she had spent the entire night in the cabin. Though her maid and the rest of the servants might wonder what had happened to her. She met Roman's gaze. "He's in London."

"Then I'll have to return there to ask for your hand." He kissed her cheek. "Will you miss me?"

"Always," she said. Then she frowned. "How did you know where to find me? I mean yesterday afternoon. I hadn't stopped at the pond as I usually do."

Roman smiled. "I went to call on you first, but the butler informed me that you had gone for a ride. I headed toward the pond to search for you. You were a good distance ahead of me, but I saw you galloping in the distance, and you had flown right by the pond. I did my best to follow you in the hope I would eventually catch up to you."

"That explains it." She hadn't thought to ask him that the day before. Another thought occurred to her. "You spoke with my sisters. What did they tell you?"

"Not much," he said. Roman paused for a moment before continuing. "What happened to send you running? They inferred that the ton was not welcoming, and you decided to end your season early."

How much should she tell him? Would it scare

him away? She should be honest with him. If they had any chance of having a good relationship, she needed to tell him the entire story. She had almost finished reading her mother's journal. "I need to show you something. Give me a minute." Athena went out to Hades and retrieved the journal from her saddlebag. Fortunately, the rain hadn't ruined it and the leather of the saddlebag had protected it from becoming waterlogged. Athena rushed back in and flipped through it. "Here, read this page."

Today I learned that my family's past will follow me wherever I go. It doesn't matter that there is no truth in the rumors or that my ancestor had been exonerated. The very fact that he had been arrested for witchcraft all those years ago still haunts the Alden family. I am an Alden first, and everyone knows that. My fear is that it will follow my daughters and their daughters. If I could save them from that possibility, I would. Isla is merely two, and soon I'll give birth to twins. There is something I have never told my husband. He would love me regardless, at least I believe he would... Nevertheless, I cannot risk seeing fear in his eyes. It would devastate me. I've seen my own death and when my twins are born, I'll never see them grow. This may be the last passage I write in here. I pray it is not. One day, they will find men to love them. I've seen that too. Fear of the future will delay the first, and temptation will be too much for one twin, and heartbreak will be another's undoing. In the end, if they choose the right path, it will lead to a happy future, and even if our family's supposed magical abilities haunt them, that love will be enough to guide them.

My daughters, if you're reading this, have faith. Believe in love, and beyond all, be true to yourselves. I love you more than anything. I have no regrets. You were my greatest gift and if I could be with you now, I would be.

Sybil, Countess of Harwood.

Roman glanced at her. "You're not a witch."

Athena stared at him. "Of course not, and neither was my mother. Though this suggests she had other special gifts. That might let others believe that she did have some magical capabilities."

"Do you think she actually saw the future?" he asked. "Is this why you ran?"

"No," she said as she shook her head. "I didn't run because of this. I hadn't even read it before I decided to leave. There was an incidence in the park and it made me afraid." She tapped the journal. "The first is delayed by fear. That is me. Though I suppose it could be Isla, too. Fear is delaying her from finding happiness, but then again, so is heartbreak." Athena shrugged. "I do know one thing. I will not let anyone scare me into rejecting happiness. I'm going to take my mother's advice and believe in our love and remain true to who I am. I won't apologize to anyone for something that is beyond my control."

"And you shouldn't have to," he agreed. "Let's get you home and then I'll go to London to speak with your father."

"Yes," she said. "It's time."

They went outside. Athena stored the journal in her saddlebag and pulled herself into the saddle. Their night together was at an end, but someday soon she'd be his wife and they would never be separated again.

Roman stayed by Athena's side as they made their way back to Harwood Hall. The manor was impressive, though not nearly as massive as the Duke of Thornridge's estate. That was to be expected, he supposed, considering Harwood was an earl and Thornridge was a higher rank. Athena led him to the stables and dismounted from her beast of a horse, then handed the reins over to a stable hand.

"Be careful when you're removing his saddle. He's a little ornerier than usual because he was tied to a post all night. I would brush him, but I'm sore myself."

"He'll be all right, my lady. Hades and I have become friends. You're still his favorite, but he'll accept me if you are not available."

"Good," Athena said. She pet Hades' mane. "I will come see you later. I promise." She turned toward Roman. He'd dismounted from his own horse and left him with another stable hand.

"I'll see you inside before I leave," he told her.

"That's unnecessary. I know my way home. It

isn't even that far from here." She winked at him, and Roman grinned.

"I'll feel better. Humor me."

"In that case," she began. "I would be happy to have you walking with me back to the manor."

She looped her arm with his and they strolled leisurely toward her home. He couldn't wait to make her his wife and have her in his home. They went inside and they both froze in the foyer. Her father was there and neither of them had expected that.

"Thank goodness," the earl said. "I arrived a half hour ago and the butler just informed me you were not here. Where have you been?" Her father glared at Roman. "Why are you together?"

Roman stared at Athena's father, uncertain what to say. Sorry, my lord, I compromised your daughter. That wouldn't go over well. The last thing he wanted to do was offend the man. Especially when he wanted to marry Athena.

"Father," Athena said. "Why are you here? I thought you would stay in London. Maeve is still participating in the season, isn't she?"

The Earl of Harwood glanced at his daughter. "The estate manager needed me here for some business. I'll return in a few days." He narrowed his gaze.

"You were riding. Did you go with him without a chaperone?"

"Of course not," she said, then snorted. "We crossed paths. I had a small fall off of Hades and the Earl of Kendal assisted me."

The concern on the Earl of Harwood's face made something inside Roman ache. He clearly adored his daughter. "Are you all right," he asked Athena. "Do you need me to send for a physician?"

"It's nothing," she reassured her father. "It hurt my pride more than anything." She glanced at Roman. "The earl was kind enough to see me home safe."

He should say something now, shouldn't he? This was as good a time as any. "My lord," he started. "If you have a moment, I'd like to speak with you."

"Of course," Harwood said. "Come with me to my study. We can speak there. I can thank you properly for assisting my daughter."

Roman glanced at Athena and smiled. "There's no need for that. I would do anything for her."

He followed the earl to his study. "It's early," Harwood began. "But I still feel like I need a drink. Would you like some brandy?"

"Yes," he answered. He needed it. Roman had never needed it more in his life.

The earl handed Roman a snifter of brandy. "What did you wish to discuss?"

Roman took a drink of the brandy. It burned as it traveled down his throat, but he welcomed it. He swirled the amber liquid in the glass and stared into it as if it held all the answers he needed. He glanced up at Harwood. "I would like to ask you for permission to marry your daughter."

Harwood grinned. "I assume you mean Athena, as I have three daughters."

A lump formed in Roman's throat. "Yes, my lord. I wish to marry Athena."

The silence in the room was deafening. Would he ever give Roman an answer? He held his breath and prayed. He wouldn't say no. Harwood couldn't be that cruel.

Harwood sipped his brandy, then set the glass on his desk. "Why do you want to marry Athena?"

That answer was easy. Roman didn't even have to think about it. "I love her."

"I trust you have heard the rumors about my late wife." Harwood held Roman's gaze. He seemed to say, without speaking a word, that Roman had better give him an answer that wasn't derogatory. The earl need not have worried.

"I don't listen to gossip," he told Harwood. "However, Athena has spoken to me about her mother and what some believe about her family. Even if there is some validity to that speculation, none of it matters to me. Athena's happiness is my only concern, and I hope I'll have the privilege of being a part of her life."

Harwood grinned. "Good answer. Yes. You may marry my daughter." The earl picked up his glass and saluted him with it. "However, it will not be a hasty wedding. The banns will be read, and it will be a proper ceremony. I do not want the ton speculating about anything and that means a special license is out of the question."

"Agreed," Roman answered. As long as she was his wife, in the end he would have agreed to any of the earl's demands.

"Now go tell my daughter she can stop listening at the door," the earl said. "And give her the news she was hoping for."

Roman smiled and did as Harwood suggested. He set his glass of brandy down. It held no interest to him any longer. Then he strode to the door and yanked it open. The earl had been right. Athena was on the other side, pacing in front of the entrance to the study. She glanced up at him and lifted one brow expectantly.

"We're going to get married," he told her. "Start planning the wedding. The banns need to be read, and I'd prefer it to be as soon as possible."

"Not too soon," Harwood yelled from behind them. "No unnecessary rumors need to spread about this union."

Athena grinned. "I think we can plan something acceptable in a couple of months. That gives us time to arrange for the banns and send out invitations."

Roman wanted to kiss her, but he knew better than to do so in front of her father. "Let's walk in the garden," he suggested. "We can discuss our wedding some more and then I'll depart to go visit my mother. She'll need to be informed of my plans to make you my countess."

She led him to toward the back entrance of the house. Once they were outside, they stopped. He pulled her into his arms and kissed her as he wanted to moments earlier. He pulled back. "I love you," he told her.

"I love you as well. Now kiss me again," she said. "You're leaving soon and I don't know when we will have a chance again."

Roman would deny her anything. Especially something he desired as well. He leaned down and pressed his lips to hers and savored her sweetness. The ton might believe she had charmed him, and perhaps she had, but he knew the truth. There was no other woman for him. They were fated. If that was magic, he would gladly thank whatever being gifted him the love of Athena. He couldn't imagine loving another as much as he adored her.

Epilogue

Three months later...

Athena stared at her husband. They had been married mere hours, but it seemed as if he had always been her husband. Roman had always been hers. She didn't know how she knew that with any amount of certainty, but she did. They were at their wedding breakfast and soon they would depart for their wedding trip. Roman still had not told her where they were going. He wanted to surprise her.

"Are you happy?" he asked.

"Yes," she told him. "As long as I am with you." She realized that not every day would be as wonderful as this one. They would disagree at times.

That was just part of life. Still, even then she would not regret marrying Roman.

"What do you make of that?" Roman gestured toward Maeve and the Viscount of Pemberton. "Does your sister know he's a rogue and should be avoided?"

Athena studied Maeve and the viscount and then smiled. She had given her mother's journal to her twin earlier that day. It was time to pass it on, and Maeve might find reading it beneficial. Athena had. "He's a temptation. My mother did say one of the twins would face it." That temptation would lead Maeve to love. The question, of course, was the viscount the temptation and did that mean Maeve would fall for him, or would he lead her to the one that she should fall for instead?

Roman sighed. "That's what I fear," he admitted. "He's my friend, but if he hurts her..."

"You do not need to worry about Maeve," she told him. "She is far more capable of protecting herself than most realize." Athena glanced at her other sister. Isla looked miserable. She kept glancing toward the Duke of Thornridge when she thought he wasn't looking. "Isla on the other hand..." She frowned. "It breaks my heart to see her so unhappy."

"Perhaps your mother was right. This time of

sorrow will lead her to where she belongs." Roman glanced at Isla. "It is terrible to witness, but some things have to be endured to find out where we belong. She will be all right in time. I have to believe that." He kissed her cheek. "During the war I experienced a lot of pain and loss, but when I made it through the worst of it I found you. This is Isla's version of that war."

Athena frowned. "I still don't like it."

"No one expects you do. That's part of living through a hardship. Nothing about it is pleasant." Roman lifted her hand and kissed her palm. "Your sisters have something few have."

"What is that?" Athena asked.

"You," he told her. "They have you, love. The three of you have a special bond that cannot be broken. So, if the worst should happen, lean on that. It will see you through almost anything."

She nodded. Athena loved her sisters, and she would help them if they should need it. If what her mother had predicted was true, they had a lot more to endure. Maeve had the lure of temptation, and apparently Isla still had a heart to mend. She didn't know who their love would end up being or what might lead them toward finding them, but she understood her sisters. They would be all right.

Athena glanced at Roman. "Thank you for loving me."

"That, my love, is my pleasure." Roman pressed his lips to hers.

Their life together was just beginning, and it was better than she could have imagined. Her destiny, her love, and and this man...she couldn't have asked for anything better.

Thank you so much for taking the time to read my book.

Your opinion matters!

Please take a moment to review this book on your favorite review site and share your opinion with fellow readers.

www.authordawnbrower.com

Excerpt: The Wallflower Identity

LADY BE VENGEFUL

Dawn Brower

The Wallflower Identity

Revenge of the Wallflowers

One

Lady Lilah Stevens was on a mission. One of great importance. At least to her... A certain viscount, one who shall remain unnamed, had ruined her. Not by actual deed, but by his damning words. If possible, she would have throttled him for being so inconsiderate. The reprobate had been foxed and slurring his words when he'd told his tale. But of course his word was above approach. Because he was a man. A man's word had to be trusted. A wallflower of little import? Not in the least...

She had hated being a wallflower, but there had been some comfort in being overlooked. Lilah had understood her place—even if it was undesirable.

No lady wished to be relegated to the sides of the dance floor. But she had accepted her unwanted identity. Lilah had been a wallflower. Emphasis on the had been part. Now she was the *infamous* wallflower. They still referred to her in her wallflower capacity, but with loud whispers and how she had taken liberties upon that infernal viscount that no *proper* young lady should have.

As if she would ever... She shuddered. Lilah did not want a scoundrel for a husband. She would much rather become a spinster and live alone for the rest of her days. If she married, she wanted to at least have mutual respect between her and her husband. How could she hold the Viscount of Harcrest in high regard when he didn't seem to have any appreciation for himself. He did not live a respectable life, and he certainly did not care how his actions affected others. In short, he was a complete arse that deserved to be punished.

Which was the reason she was about to meet with her fellow wallflowers. They had made a pact. One that would ensure that each of their acts of revenge would be successful. They were all wallflowers. No one noticed them. That was the beauty of being a wallflower, or at least it had been. Now that she was notorious everything had changed.

Lilah did not have the luxury of hiding in the shadows any longer. She would have to depend upon her friends to aid her cause.

They were meeting at Hyde Park. Not during the fashionable hour of course. They did not wish for anyone to witness their gathering. A wallflower might go unnoticed, but someone might comment upon Lilah being in the park. Many gentlemen kept their distance from her when she was in their general vicinity. As if she might accost them in some fashion. Because of this she'd become resigned. There was no helping her situation now. Lilah would be a spinster, and she'd accept that fate. After, she taught that bloody viscount a much-needed lesson anyway.

"Must you walk so fast," Cora, her sister, asked, a little breathlessly. "I can barely keep up with you." Cora was older than her by a year and also a fellow wallflower. This wasn't her first season, and it may be her last as well. Unfortunately, Lilah's new reputation flowed downhill to the rest of her family. She still had not spoken directly to her father about the incident.

"My apologies," Lilah said. "I'm just so...errr." She opened and closed her fingers into fists. "I want to hit him." It would not solve anything, but it would feel good to release some of her pent up frustration.

It had been merely a sennight since he's callously ruined her. She still wondered why he'd done it. What had she done to him to make him think speak so ill of her? If only she could understand his reasoning. Perhaps then she might not be quite so angry with him. Lilah considered it... No, she would still be livid. But that didn't mean she did not still wish to understand the rotten scoundrel's motives.

"And you have every right to that anger," Cora said. "We all understand it. However, please do not take it out on me. I'd like to be able to walk home later. At this pace, I'll be exhausted before we reach the park." Cora tucked a strand of her black hair behind her ear. Her brown eyes were filled with concern as she gazed upon her. She was correct. Cora hadn't been the one to cause her harm and she shouldn't take it out on her.

Lilah sighed and slowed her pace. They didn't live too far from Hyde Park, and before her reputation had been ruined, they had gone there during the fashionable hour often. They enjoyed going to the park. Now it was almost impossible for them to go anywhere without whispers following them. "I truly am sorry," she told Cora. "I'll endeavor to not take out my frustrations on you. Forgive me?"

"Of course, sister dear," Cora told her. "I'm here for you. As is Victoria, Emma, and Selena."

Emma was the true surprise. Her brother was the blasted viscount that had ruined Lilah's good name. She had fully expected Emma would bow out on this scheme. But she'd said her brother should have known better and someone should show him the error of his ways. For that reason alone, Lilah adored the woman. As wallflowers, they had all known each other existed. One didn't hug a wall all season and not notice the rest of the ladies being ignored. However, they hadn't truly talked until that fateful evening of Lilah's ruination. In was then they had made their pact. They all had reasons for enacting a plot of revenge, and by the end of the year, they intended to see them fulfilled.

Lilah's would be first. Depending on its success, they would move on to the next wallflower. They still had not decided which one of the ladies would be next. After Lilah got her revenge, they would make that decision. "I'm grateful to all of you."

"I still cannot believe Lord Harcrest said all of that." She shook her head and sighed. "And we have already discussed this ad nauseam. We don't need to do so again. I'm sorry."

"You have nothing to apologize for," Lilah told her. "You're not the one that wronged me." They reached Hyde Park and headed to the area they had agreed to meet. There was a tall shade tree at the back of the park close to the Serpentine that would be perfect. It was only noon, and they had much to discuss before the fashionable hour. They did not wish to be in the park when everyone started to make their appearances. They had roughly four hours. Not that she thought they would need that long.

"There they are," Cora said, and gestured in the other ladies direction.

Victoria, Selena, and Emma were sitting on a blanket under the tree. They had brought a picnic basket so they could eat while they talked. Lilah's stomach growled as if on cue. She hadn't realized how hungry she had gotten. Her anger had masked it as they walked.

They hurried over to the other women. They had brought a blanket as well. Cora spread it out, and they both sat down on it. "Now that we are all here," Lilah began. "Has anyone thought about what we should do?"

"I have," Emma said. She twirled a stray blonde lock as she stared at Lilah. "It is the only thing I can think of that would both terrify and anger my brother."

That piqued Lilah's interest. "And what would that be?" Whatever it was, she would see it happen. That man had to pay for what he'd done to her.

"He needs to wed," Emma said.

Lilah wrinkled her nose in displeasure. She'd thought she'd do anything, but apparently she had a line she would not cross. "I am not marrying your brother."

Emma laughed. "And it's understandable that you do not wish to be tied to him forever. What he did to you is bloody awful." She held up a hand. "But please listen to what I have to say. You don't have to be the one marrying him. But we can ensure that he is trapped, nonetheless." She shrugged nonchalantly. "My brother should have married by now. In a way, I'm doing him a favor."

"And who would the unlucky lady be?" She wasn't certain she wanted to tie any woman to him, and she didn't question Emma's last statement either—that was none of her business. What woman would deserve to be his wife? Lilah couldn't think of one. "And why is this a deserving punishment?"

"Because he has boasted on several occasions he will never marry," Emma said. "For any reason and to any woman. He has even said that he didn't care if he was caught in a scandalous fashion with a woman. He would not marry her." Emma sighed. "He has a duty to his title; however, he refuses to accept that and find a wife."

"Then how are we going to force his hand?" Lilah wasn't so certain this would work.

"That's easy," Selena said. "We put a woman in his path that he can't refuse."

"But Emma just said..." Lilah was so confused.

"My brother may think he can refuse any woman, but we all know that isn't true. There are ladies that have fathers or older brothers that will ensure he's at the altar and saying those vows."

She was right. "Unless he wants to find himself in a duel of some sort, that is true." Lilah turned toward Emma. "Would he risk that?"

She shook her head. "My brother's honor is questionable, and he values his life too much to risk it in a duel. He'd rather marry than face death." Emma grinned. "And that will be his undoing. Truly, this is for the best. For everyone." She had a faraway expression on her face that made Lilah wonder what Emma hadn't said.

Lilah didn't have a father or brother willing to fight a duel for her. Her father was too old to take such a risk. Not that she wanted to marry Lord Harcrest. Lilah wanted the impossible—her bloody reputation back. "Then what is the plan?"

"And that's my cue," Victoria chimed in. Lady Victoria Spencer had brown hair and hazel eyes. She was curvy and beautiful. "I have convinced my brother we must have a house party, and only the best guests are invited." She popped a chunk of cheese into her mouth and chewed. "Which means you will all be there, of course." She motioned toward Emma. "And that scoundrel brother of yours will have to escort you there. So, he'll be in attendance."

"Indeed," Emma agreed.

"Now," Lady Selena Brooks began. "As to Lord Harcrest's potential bride." Her blue eyes gleamed with amusement. Her golden-brown hair was pulled into an elegant chignon, not a hair out of place. She was a true beauty and her wallflower status shocking to them all. Unless one knew about the dire straits her family had been in. Her brother had turned the tables on their fortune, but that hadn't saved Selena in time when she was launched into society. She had a dowry now that rivaled some of the wealthier families, but she didn't let that secret out. If a man only wanted her for her money, then she wanted nothing to do with them. "I have a few ladies on my list that will be perfect. One is the daughter of a duke and is beyond haughty. I cannot count how many times she's turned up her nose at me."

"As the daughter of a duke she'll have a good dowry. Does Lord Harcrest deserve a rich wife?" Cora asked.

"Normally I would agree with you," Selena said. "But for this to work, we have to pick a lady that will be formidable, and that her family will protect at all costs. That means money. For some, their reputation means more than their coffers. Well, to a certain extent."

"That's true," Lilah said. "It's not a perfect solution, but you know either way the viscount will hate being forced to wed anyone."

"Absolutely," Emma said. She turned her head thoughtfully, as if considering her next words carefully. "Trust me. My brother will fight this to the bitter end. But when it is all said and done, he will not have a choice. He'll accept his fate, even if he resents it."

"So is this what we're going to do?" Victoria asked. "I've already insisted on this house party. My brother didn't like the idea, but he's agreed."

"I believe it is our best choice," Lilah said. "It doesn't seem enough, though."

"Well," Emma began. "We can also slowly torture him while we are at the house party. Play little tricks on him. You know, like small children do to their governess." She grinned mischievously. "I've always wanted to play pranks on him."

"Oh," Cora said. "I like that. We will have to come up with a few awful things to do to him. I'll start a list when we return home."

That was Cora, always making lists. "You all are the best. Thank you for helping me with this," Lilah said, gratitude evident in her tone as she spoke.

"It is our pleasure," Selena told her. "He deserves this. He will learn that it is never a good idea to ruin a woman. Especially without cause."

"One would hope..." Lilah blew out a breath. "But clearly, he's not one that thinks before he acts. He may never truly learn anything."

Emma shrugged. "He will pay for his actions. We'll have to accept that and live with it." Her lips twitched. "And I'll start this out with something that will guarantee to get his attention. It'll lay the groundwork for our little scheme."

"And what is that?" Selena asked.

"He started a scandal that spread rumors faster than we can blink," Emma said. "We're going to use that to our advantage. Give a few of the more reliable gossips something to that'll gladly spread around."

"What did you have in mind?" Lilah asked with interest.

"Let it be known that one Viscount Harcrest is ready to wed and that all interested parties be prepared to present themselves for consideration." She winked. "That way when he is caught inflagranti delicto at the house party it won't be such a surprise to him that a lady tried to catch his interest."

"That's rich. Considering how much he's made it known he'll never marry." Emma grinned. "I like it. This is going to be fun." She rubbed her hands with glee. "I know, I'm terrible. This is my brother we're discussing. It really is for his own good, though. The title does need an heir and he will never do it on his own. I'm helping. Truly."

"You do not need to convince us," Selena said,

then shrugged. "We all want this to succeed." She grinned too. "And you're right. This is going to be fun."

She nodded. This was what they were going to do. They had a plan. Now they just had to ensure it all went smoothly. In approximately a fortnight, the viscount would understand how wrong he'd been. At least that was the hope...

Two

Henry Collins, the Viscount of Harcrest, scrolled into his club whistling as he walked. His day could not have gone better if he'd actually tried to make it so. He'd stayed up all night gambling in a den of iniquity that had proved profitable.

Now that he'd had a little bit of rest, he was about to meet with a few of his friends. This club wasn't filled with everything sinful, but it still catered to gentlemen that wished to gather free of scrutiny. He preferred the other type of place, but this club had its uses.

He walked into the backroom to find four of his closest friends already there waiting for him. They were at a table drinking what he could only assume was brandy. The Earl of Foxcroft lifted his glass and took a long swig. Before his father died and he'd inherited the title, he'd been one of Henry's closest friends. He would have been right by his side as they spent the night in every sinful activity they could find. That had changed when he had to take on so much more responsibility. It didn't help that his father had left the earldom near penniless and creditors nearly knocking down his door. Henry had to commend Foxcroft for pulling his family from the brink of ruin.

"Hello all," Henry said as he took a seat at the table. He turned to the Earl of Thornton on his left. "Surprised to see you here, Ole' chap," he said. "I thought you abhorred the club."

"I hate a lot of things that I'm forced to endure," Thornton said dryly. He ran a hand through his black hair, leaving it disheveled. "But even I have to leave my house from time to time." He gestured toward the Duke of Castlebury. "His Grace thought this should be one of those times."

The duke glared at Thornton. They had similar black hair, but their eyes were different. Where Thornton's were green, Castlebury's were blue. Rumors suggested they were truly brothers, and that Thornton was one of Castlebury's father's by-blows. No one knew for certain, but Castlebury's connection to him didn't help the rumors from spreading. They were too close, and some questioned Thornton's right to the earldom. His father never disowned him. He held the title—even if most believed he was actually a bastard. Henry had never asked. He didn't think it was his business, although he did have a bit of curiosity. He wouldn't turn the information away if it presented itself. Though he did know that Thornton's father had always been hard on him and that was one reason he didn't socialize much.

"Thornton spends too much time in his study brooding," Castlebury said. "You would think he'd have some motivation to enjoy life now that he's able to."

"Because my father's dead?" Thornton asked. "Let's all toast to the rotten old codger," he said as he lifted his glass of brandy. "May he continue to burn in hell." Definitely no love lost there...

The Marquess of Ardmore shook his head. "Mate," he began. "I feel for you, but at least you no longer have to live with the man." He wasn't even certain why Ardmore had decided to join them. It took a lot to catch his interest. This club wouldn't normally top that any of the marquess's lists.

"Why are you with us this evening Ardmore," Henry asked, his curiosity getting the better of him. "Nothing more appealing for you this evening?"

He sighed. "You're as uncouth as usual, Harcrest." Ardmore sipped his brandy. "But if you must know, I do have another engagement." His lips twitched in amusement. "But not until much later. Until then, you chaps will have to suffice."

"How kind of you to grace us with your presence?" Henry rolled his eyes.

"By the way," Ardmore began. "I'm having a house party in a fortnight. You're all invited." He said it so nonchalantly it gave Henry pause. The marquess did not have house parties.

"And why would we want to attend a house party?" The duke drawled. "That sounds positively dreadful." His tone suggested it would be far more than that, and he would rather not attend.

"As His Grace has so eloquently stated," Henry said. "House parties are not the sort of entertainment we seek out."

"That is why this one will be far more interesting than most," Ardmore said, and then winked. "Would I have a party that promised nothing but ennui?"

Well, when he put it that way... "I've never

known you to be dull." The marquess did have a certain reputation.

"Is this a house party that promises debauchery?" Henry would absolutely attend, if that were the case. It had been an age when he'd attended a party of that sort.

"Of course not." Ardmore rolled his eyes. "My little sister will be there. That's not the proper environment for a young lady." He sighed. "But I will have some private entertainments at a hunting lodge on my property. For those with more... discerning tastes."

Henry grinned. "All right," he said in a jovial tone. "You've convinced me." He was curious enough to go and discover what the marquess had planned.

"I'll consider it," the duke said. "Depends on what other entertainments are available. I rarely enjoy the country."

"Do you enjoy anything?" Thornton asked?

"Do you?" Castlebury retorted. They glared at each other for several excruciating moments.

"Well," Foxcroft said. "Now that we've moved past that uncomfortable exchange..." He lifted his brandy and gestured toward the marquess. "I'll be there. Whether these two leave London or not. So you'll have two of us at your private party while the rest of your guest take over your house."

Ardmore laughed. "That aspect of the party is all Victoria," he said. "My sister decided that she wanted to gather with a few of her friends and coerced me into this party. She's inviting others, so it should be a grand affair." He rolled his eyes. "It'll be a pain, but if you're all there, it will be more tolerable."

"Well," Foxcroft said. "If the betting book is accurate, it should be an opportunity for Harcrest here."

"I don't follow," Harcrest said. What the blazes was Foxcroft going on about? "What's in the betting book?" He had a terrible feeling he would not like what he had to say next.

"That you're officially in the market for a wife," Foxcroft said.

Henry blinked. Several times. Did he just say...

"You are?" The duke spun to look at him. "Since when?"

"I bloody well am not," Harcrest sputtered out. "What the bloody hell... That cannot be correct."

He had to go take a gander at that book. Who would have started that rumor? Why was it even in the betting books? Whoever had done this was going to hear from him. This was horrid. If the ton at large heard that rumor... Then he'd be pursued for the purpose of marriage. He shuddered in horror. He had carefully cultivated his reputation to avoid that.

"I assure you," Foxcroft said in a smooth tone. "It is definitely in the books. The wagers vary in what they think will happen. The odds do not favor you my friend. Most believe that some adventurous young lady will win your hand by the end of the summer."

"Bollocks," he cursed. "I don't understand any of this. Why are they even making these bets?"

"Perhaps it has something to do with your drunken behavior at that ball a sennight ago." It was almost the end of the season and a lot of families would be returning to the country for the summer. That was probably why Ardmore was having his house party in a fortnight.

"Again, I do not understand. As I was inebriated, my memory is lacking. Please explain." Harcrest rubbed his temples. Perhaps he should stop imbibing so much. No, that wouldn't solve anything, and he enjoyed brandy.

"You claimed a pretty little wallflower tried to strip you and have her wicked way with you."

Ardmore wiggled his eyebrows suggestively. "And that she was quite determined in her pursuit."

"A wallflower?" That also seemed implausible. "Why would a wallflower try to take off my clothes?" And more importantly, what was her name? Was she indeed pretty, and if so, why was she a wallflower? He had more questions than answers.

"That is the question on almost everyone's lips," Foxcroft said.

"I cannot help wondering myself," the duke drawled. "I've seen Lady Lilah Stephens. She is indeed pretty. On the poorer side, but lovely none-theless. Not as pretty as some of the other debu-tantes this season. Probably why she was mostly ignored. There were far more appealing prospects. That is, if one was in the market for a wife."

"Which you are not," Henry supplied.

"Quite true, mate," he said. The duke downed his brandy and then poured more into his glass. "Much like we all believed of you. But since that night a sennight ago many have wondered if perhaps you were just looking for a reason to claim the chit. I mean, you ruined her with your tale. Are you certain you do not recall this?"

He frowned. He didn't even recall going to a ball. Could it have happened? Why would he tell everyone that she'd accosted him if she hadn't actually done it? "Do you know whether or not it was true?"

"That's what everyone believes," Foxcroft said. "However, I do not know if Lady Lilah Stephens actually did the deeds you claimed." He shrugged. "No one witnessed these acts. But your words did enough damage that the lady is practically ostracized."

"I don't remember..." Henry rubbed his hand over his face. If he did say all of it, and the lady did not in fact try to remove his clothes... What had he done? He had to find out if it was true and somehow fix it. The lady should not be shunned because of his drunken stupidity. However, if she had tried to do as he claimed, perhaps she has gotten what she deserved.

"My sister is friends with her," Ardmore said in a casual tone. "I didn't like it, but she plans on inviting her to the house party. You can rest assured that she won't even come close to you during the party." He met Henry's gaze. "The lady hates you and will avoid you. There might be other ladies that would willingly trap you into marriage, but Lady Lilah won't be amongst their ranks."

"Well, hell...." He had a lot to make amends for,

apparently. "I don't even know her. Why would I say all of that?"

"I cannot say with any certainty," Foxcroft told him. "We have all wondered it ourselves." He motioned between himself, Ardmore, the duke, and Thornton. "But the real question is. Are you really looking for a wife?"

"No," he said emphatically. "That has not changed. If you want to place a wager, then I'd bet against everyone else."

"Oh, I already placed my wager," Foxcroft said. "I am leaning toward you, finding yourself leg shackled. There will be some determined young lady that makes it her mission to be your wife, and you'll find yourself in a neat little parson's trap."

"You're an arse." Henry glared at him.

"But I'm right," he said. "The remaining unmarried ladies after this season's end will look at you as their last chance. They will circle you like you're their prey and it's their last meal."

He shuddered. "God..." What an image that was in his head now. "Maybe I shouldn't attend this house party after all."

"Awfully cowardly of you," the duke said, then laughed. "But that is to be expected."

"You would hide if you were in a similar position," Henry exclaimed.

"I am already," the duke told him. "Every damn day. It doesn't matter how much I claim that I do not wish to wed. Some young lady with high aspirations of becoming a duchess will get a grand idea of how to trap me or make me love her. It's the curse of being a duke." He shrugged. "You could only live on that awful reputation of yours for so long. This was bound to happen. It was only a matter of time."

Henry hated that his friend was right. But that did not mean he had to like it. "Well," he said. "I guess I'll still attend. However, I have lost any interest in doing anything more this evening. If you'll pardon me, I am going home." He would drown his sorrows in his own brandy in the safety of home. Then he'd ponder all the mistakes he had made and decide what he should do next. What a bloody mess... "Good evening." With those words, he stood and left his club. His mood soured, and his mind troubled.

ORDER HERE: https://books2read.com/ WallflowerIdentity

Excerpt: Rogue Wallflower

LADY BE VENGEFUL

Lady Victoria Spencer has loved one man her entire life. Of course he never notices her. Why should he? She's a wallflower and no one pays the unwanted ladies much mind. Had she been a bit plump? Yes. Now that she no longer is, she has a plan. She's going to become a rogue wallflower, and only one man will do as her first lover.

David Brooks, Earl of Foxcroft had led a charmed life. Right up until his father died and he was forced to take responsibility for his family and the estates. His father had run the coffers nearly empty and it had been up to him to restore their fortune. He could have married an heiress, but felt that was a cowardly way out. Instead he focused on rebuilding his fortune. Now that he feels secure enough with his family's status he has decided to take a wife. Only one woman will do, but now that he can claim her would rather take a lover, not a husband.

All Victoria needs is a gentleman well versed in everything roguish to give her those lessons. David seizes upon the opportunity. He is more than willing to use her curiosity to his advantage. As long as in the end, he's the only rogue she completes those skills with.

Order Here: https://books2read.com/ RogueWallflower

Prologue

❧

Lady Cora Stephens happily wandered through the garden at her father's, the Earl of Farrington's country home. She loved the garden and spent as much time as possible there during the summer months. Cora could not imagine a more perfect place, and in her heart, she never wanted to call any other place hers. At ten and two, she could not imagine anything else. She wanted Farrington Abbey to always be her home. She stopped at her favorite area of the garden. In the center of the path was a large fountain with a sculpture of a one of the Greek goddesses regally overlooking the garden. She did not know which goddess claimed this part of the garden, she just believed her lovely, strong, and brave. Cora wanted to be all three of those, and perhaps one day she would be so fortunate.

"Of course you're here," a boy said from the other side of the fountain. "You're always here."

She glared at him. Hayes Grant, the future Earl of Thornton, and the current Viscount Beaxton, was her nemesis. For as long as she could recall, he had been spending summers at her home, and before he'd been sent to Eton, he'd been at her home more often than his. He wasn't even a blood relation. She did not understand why her father wanted the horrid boy around. He was four years older than her, and always a nuisance. "This is my home." She glared at him. "If you do not wish to be in my company, then perhaps you should go back to yours."

He sneered at her. "Trust me, little urchin. I'd rather be anywhere than here."

She'd always hated him. Her father doted on him as if he were perfect. Clearly, her father had never seen how Viscount Beaxton treated his eldest daughter. If he had, then he might not want the horrid boy around. Though he wasn't merely a boy any longer. He'd turn six and ten a few months past.

She stared at him and studied the changes. He was still a little gangly—too thin. She wondered why. Did he not eat enough? His dark hair was on the longer side and seemed to almost gleam in sunlight. His green eyes though... That was his best feature. They reminded her of leaves at the start of spring. All new and sprouting toward the sunshine while they grew for the upcoming summer months. Not that dark green of a fully formed leaf, but the light shade of a new spring bud.

Cora didn't like that she noticed these things about him. She didn't want to find something, anything, about him appealing. She wanted to continue to hate him and enjoy the peace in that fact. He was a pretty boy, and one day he would probably be a devastating man. One with the power to break a lady's heart. She would not be that lady. Cora could never love a man that treated her as inconsequential. He seemed to hate her as much as she loathed him. They were comfortable in their dislike of each other, and she doubted that would ever change.

"Then why come at all?" she asked him as she forced herself out of her revery. "We both would be far happier if we didn't have to cross paths."

"If it were my choice," he began. "I'd never gaze upon you again."

Was she that horrid to behold? Cora didn't think herself ugly, but she was a mere girl. Her hair was as dark as his, but her eyes were not a lovely shade of green. They were a boring brown. "There is a sentiment I can agree with." She lifted her chin defiantly. "I'd rather not see you, either."

"You're unbearable." He narrowed his gaze, then brushed past her, causing her to lose her balance. She tumbled toward the fountain with an alarming speed. Cora flailed her arms, attempting to right herself, but to no avail. Before she knew it, she'd fallen into the water face first. She came up sputtering and spitting out water. Her gown was drenched and completely ruined. Lord Dalton glanced at her and then laughed. "Now that," he said between chuckles. "Is well worth the lengthy journey to visit this insufferable estate. I must thank you for keeping me entertained."

"ohhh," she said in frustration. Cora glared at him. "This is all your fault. You pushed me."

"I did not." He shrugged nonchalantly. "But I could have been more careful. Though now that I have witnessed the results, I must admit. I don't regret my negligence." The smug expression on his face grated on her bruised ego.

That did it. He had to pay for being such an obnoxious lout. Before she thought about her actions, Cora stormed over to him and then pushed him. He tumbled backward into the fountain. When he came up sputtering water as she had earlier, she laughed. With a grin, she admitted, "You're right, Lord Beast. That was nothing but pure joy to behold." Cora curtsied. "I'll take your leave now. I'm certain you can find your own way out of the fountain. Much as I had to mere moments ago."

"That is not my name," he shouted at her.

Cora shrugged as if he didn't matter. Because at that moment, he didn't. She did not stop to look back as she made her way back to the house. Her father would likely chastise her later for her behavior, but she couldn't make herself care. It had been worth it to see him a drenched mess and fluttering around in the fountain. The viscount hadn't helped her. He'd laughed. Shouldn't she repay him in kind?

She didn't want to hate him, but he made it impossible to do anything else. When he'd come to Farrington Abbey for the first time, she'd believed he would be her friend. How wrong she'd been. Instead, he had become her enemy and nothing had changed that in all these years. They would always be this way with each other. Some things could not be changed and no amount of wishing could alter that.

ORDER HERE: https://books2read.com/ RogueWallflower

Excerpt: Her Duke to Savor

❧

LADY BE WICKED

Elias Stevens, the Marquess of Savorton doesn't believe he'll ever fall in love. He may marry one day, because the title demands it; however, that elusive emotion will not be freely given to his future wife.

A house party changes everything for him though. His dearest friend makes a wager with him. He'll fall in love by the new year. Elias takes that bet because he knows his own heart.

Lady Gabriella St. Giles lives a charmed life. She has a good family and fully believes one day she'll mean a gentleman sure to steal her heart. What she doesn't count on is meeting an unsavory marquess at a house party.

Love is on the agenda. One of them wants it and the other hopes to desperately escape it. That wager gives the marquess far more than he could ever imagined, and Gabriella may just acquire her own future duke to savor.

Prologue

E lias Stevens, the Marquess of Savorton, leaned in his chair and then rocked it on the back two legs as he studied his cards. How many should he discard? After pondering it for a few moments, he set his chair back down on all four legs and leaned on the table. He plucked five cards out of his hand and placed them face down on the table, and then drew five more from the deck carefully arranging them with the ones he still held.

He refrained from grinning at the cards he'd added to his hand. He glanced up at his dearest friend, Elena, the Dowager Countess of Dryden. Her dark red hair shimmered in the candlelight, and there was a gleam in her light gray eyes. She was studying her own cards. The two of them were engrossed in a duel of sorts as they played a grueling game of piquet. This was their last hand in a set of six and would determine which one of them came out the winner. It was a close game and either of them might be declared the victor.

"It's your turn, love," Eli reminded her and tapped a finger impatiently on the table.

"I'm aware," she drawled. "I do not need your guidance." Elena winked. "I'm a far better player than you are."

"Debatable," he replied in an arrogant tone. "I am not so certain you're correct."

Her lips lifted into one of her sensual smiles. It was the type of smile that would set most men aflame with desire, but Eli felt nothing. For him that smile meant something far different. The minx was about to pounce and he would end up metaphorically wounded after she made her strike. Hell. She was going to win, and he didn't like it.

"You always did hate losing," she replied in a glib tone. She removed three cards from her hand and then replaced them with three more from the deck. "There's no need for deliberations. We both know the truth."

"That piquet is a game of chance?" Eli lifted a

brow. "In that you are correct." He refused to admit defeat until he absolutely had to.

She laughed and then grinned at him. "I suppose that is true with any game used for the purpose of gambling. Luck may or may not be on your side." She rearranged her cards in her hand. "But we both know piquet is much more than that. It requires skill, strategy, and an excellent memory. I happen to have all three."

Eli shook his head and sighed and made his declarations, and they continued on with the game. After they were done playing, he had to confess, "I concede, you won." He met her gaze. "I'm not saying you are a better player though."

"Of course you will not. I'd expect nothing less." Her gray eyes sparkled with mischief. "You never have. Why would you change that core part of you now?"

They were at Elena's London townhouse. Many members of the ton believed they were lovers, but nothing could be farther from the truth. Elena and Eli had been friends since they were children. He was only three years older than her, and they first met when he was four and she could barely stand to walk in the nursery. Their mothers had been close and that had brought them together often. Eli was as protective of Elena as he would be if he'd had a sister. When she had married an old man, he had tried to persuade her against the match, but she reminded him they all had their duties to perform and her marriage landed firmly in that column. Her father had arranged the marriage, and she had done as she was told.

Elena had regretted it as her marriage made her miserable. Her husband hadn't been abusive, exactly, but he'd been cold. When she failed to conceive, he'd treated her as if she were a useless person. He may never have physically hit her, but his words were like blows that failed to leave a visible bruise. Eli had never been happier when the earl ceased breathing. When the Earl of Dryden dropped dead suddenly Eli had rejoiced, and secretly so had Elena.

"Do you think you'll ever remarry?" he asked in a noncommittal tone.

She snorted. "Not bloody likely. One marriage of inconvenience is enough to turn me away from such an endeavor." Elena gathered the cards and stacked them neatly on the table. "Why do you ask?"

He didn't want to tell her he'd been thinking about how unhappy she had been. Elena enjoyed being a widow. She had freedom and if she wanted a lover, she could and probably had taken one. Not that, to his knowledge, she did... Eli didn't ask her about anything he didn't really want answers to. "What if you fell in love?"

"That is even more unlikely. Love is a myth they try to make a woman believe." She leaned back and studied him. "Are you in love, Eli?"

"Absolutely not," he said in an emphatic tone. "Unless you count that gorgeous opera singer, I spent an evening with a few nights ago. She was delicious and might convince me I could believe in love."

He was far too busy helping build Savorton Shipping. His family had struggled when he was younger and now that he could, he worked to make their fortune something that rivaled even the most affluent in English society. He was an heir to a dukedom and now the estate thrived. His father had become frail in his old age and left running all the estates to Eli, but still offered input when he felt it was required. Eli did not have time for love.

"A night of passion is not love," Elena replied in a dry tone. "Neither of us is on the market for that elusive emotion."

"So you do not believe you will ever willingly give your heart away?" This seemed like an opportunity. Should he take it? Elena had never really given any man a chance, and she had good reason for that. As a widow of wealthy means, she didn't have to remarry, but she had a past she seemed determined to forget. One he wanted to remind her about in a subtle way. "You don't have to marry a man if you love him, you know."

"I'm aware," she said, then tilted her head to the side. "I never have to marry again. But you do."

"I've never been married, love," he replied. "I cannot marry again when I never have."

"You are purposely misunderstanding me," she accused. "You know perfectly well what I meant. You're going to be a duke one day and you need heirs."

"I was hoping to convince you to marry me," he said in a smooth tone. "You're the only woman I actually like."

"What a vile thing to suggest." She glared at him. "The very idea of sharing a bed with you..." Elena shuddered.

"Now that wasn't necessary. I'm not revolting." He frowned. She made a valid argument, though. Eli didn't wish to bed her any more than she wanted to join him in that activity.

"Darling," she began as she studied him. "You

are passably handsome. I've heard many debutantes expound on your breathtaking visage. Apparently, your black hair and green eyes make them swoon with desire."

"Of course, they do. What they actually desire to be a future duchess, and my gorgeous physique has nothing to do with their admiration." Eli might be a bit jaded... "I am not marrying until I absolutely have to, and love won't be part of the bargain."

"That's too bad," she said in a somber tone. "You're destined to have a marriage like mine."

"I won't be a brute like your husband was. I'd never treat a woman so callously." He wouldn't. Eli had to believe he'd be better than the late Earl of Dryden. Elena was still young and only eight and twenty. She could find someone to be happy with. Somehow, he had to convince her to try.

"Perhaps not," she agreed. "You might be the one that is emotionally abused. I pray you choose wisely."

"I'll have you approve of my future wife." He smiled. "You may have better judgement than me."

"I already do," she said, then laughed. "Perhaps we should make a wager."

It couldn't be that easy... She was playing right

into his plans. Elena was a lot like him. She hated to lose. "What sort of wager?"

She tapped on the cards. "All gambling is a matter of chance, but some games are a little more than that. Much like piquet, love can be played in a similar fashion."

"So we use our strategy and skill to avoid falling?" he asked, trying to understand her meaning.

"In a sense," she replied. "We will also have to keep track of all the players, for unlike our little game here, there will be more than two."

"And what exactly is this wager?" Eli asked.

"How about we make it simple," she began. "The first to fall in love by the end of Christmastide loses and owes the other a boon."

He pondered her suggestion. "And what if neither of us falls?"

"Then we both win," she said in a wistful tone. "Or perhaps we will both lose, depending on one's perspective."

Eli doubted he would fall in love. He had yet to meet a woman that inspired such an insipid emotion in him. "All right, I accept. In fact, I have the perfect playing field for us."

She lifted a brow. "Oh?"

"Lady Winston is having a house party. It begins

in a couple of weeks and will extend through the entirety of Christmastide. My mother has been hounding me to attend. I'll tell her I will as long as you go and we can put our wager to the test."

Elena steepled her fingers together. "Excellent," she said in a gleeful tone. "Let the best player win, then."

He was going to enjoy watching her fall, for he knew something she did not. The Earl of Northfield would be in attendance. Elena had never said as much, but the earl had been her first and only love. One she had never had a chance at having a relationship with. Elena had shoved those feelings deep inside her and prepared to marry the Earl of Dryden as her father had ordered. Perhaps this was her second chance at finding happiness.

He wasn't worried about himself. Eli had time to find a suitable wife. His concern was for his dearest friend and helping her find a love she deserved. Besides he hadn't lied, Eli didn't believe in love, at least not when it came to his own life. Love was for other people. Individuals who had the luxury of accepting that gift into their lives. Eli would never be that fortunate.

Acknowledgments

To all my readers. I appreciate you more than I can ever convey. I hope you enjoy this series, and the many more I have planned for you.

About Dawn Brower

USA TODAY Bestselling author, DAWN BROWER writes both historical and contemporary romance. There are always stories inside her head; she just never thought she could make them come to life. That creativity has finally found an outlet.

Growing up, she was the only girl out of six children. She raised two boys as a single mother; there is never a dull moment in her life. Reading books is her favorite hobby, and she loves all genres.

www.authordawnbrower.com
TikTok: @1DawnBrower

BB bookbub.com/authors/dawn-brower
f facebook.com/1DawnBrower
X x.com/1DawnBrower
instagram.com/1DawnBrower
g goodreads.com/dawnbrower

Also by Dawn Brower

Loving an America Spy

Linked Across Time

Saved by My Blackguard

Searching for My Rogue

Seduction of My Rake

Surrendering to My Spy

Spellbound by My Charmer

Stolen by My Knave

Separated from My Love

Scheming with My Duke

Secluded with My Hellion

Secrets of My Beloved

Spying on My Scoundrel

Shocked by My Vixen

Smitten with My Christmas Minx

Vision of Love

Enduring Legacy

The Legacy's Origin

Charming Her Rogue

Ever Beloved

Forever My Earl

Always My Viscount

Infinitely My Marquess

Eternally My Duke

Bluestockings Defying Rogues

When An Earl Turns Wicked

A Lady Hoyden's Secret

One Wicked Kiss

Earl In Trouble

All the Ladies Love Coventry

One Less Scandalous Earl

Confessions of a Hellion

The Vixen in Red

Lady Pear's Duke

Scandal Meets Love

Love Only Me (Amanda Mariel)

Find Me Love (Dawn Brower)

If It's Love (Amanda Mariel)

Odds of Love (Dawn Brower)

Believe In Love (Amanda Mariel)

Chance of Love (Dawn Brower)

Love and Holly (Amanda Mariel)

Love and Mistletoe (Dawn Brower

The Neverhartts

Never Defy a Vixen

Never Disregard a Wallflower

Never Dare a Hellion

Never Deceive a Bluestocking

Never Disrespect a Governess

Never Desire a Duke

Lady Be Wicked/Wayward Dukes'/Wicked Widows'

Her Rogue for One Night (Wicked Widows)

A Lady Never Tells

Her Duke to Beguile

Her Duke of Sin (Wayward Dukes')

Her Duke to Savor (Wayward Dukes')

Coming in 2024/2025

A Lady Never Confesses

A Lady Never Forgets

Her Rogue for Christmas (Wicked Widows)

Her Rogue to Kiss Good Morning (Wicked Widows)

Her Duke to Seduce (Wayward Dukes')

Her Duke to Tempt (Wayward Dukes')

CONTEMPORARY

Stand alone:

Deadly Benevolence

Snowflake Kisses

Kindred Lies

Sparkle City

Diamonds Don't Cry

Hooking a Firefly

Novak Springs

Cowgirl Fever

Dirty Proof

Unbridled Pursuit

Sensual Games

Christmas Temptation

Daring Love

Passion and Lies

Desire and Jealousy

Seduction and Betrayal

Begin Again

There You'll Be

Better as a Memory

Won't Let Go

Heart's Intent

One Heart to Give

Unveiled Hearts

Excerpt: Her Duke of Sin

WAYWARD DUKES' ALLIANCE

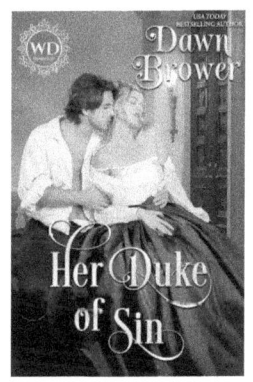

Excerpt: Her Duke of Sin

WAYWARD DUKES' ALLIANCE

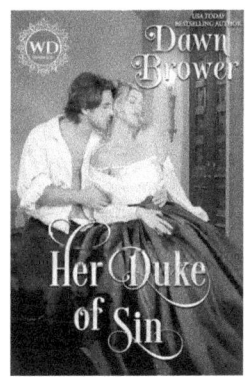

Prologue

Miss Juliet Adams pulled her cloak tight around herself. She shivered as an icy wind blew through her. Her cloak had seen better days and offered little in the way of warmth. Everything she owned was at least three years old and ill fitting. She could not remember the last time she'd had an update in her wardrobe. It had definitely been before her father had become bedridden, and since his death her situation had taken an even more dire turn.

This was her last chance. She had nowhere else to go. If she didn't obtain this position, she didn't know where she might end up. Juliet feared she might have to do things she never imagined possible. Truthfully, she had already gone down that path to some degree. Soon she'd be forced to beg for food and pray she didn't freeze to death on the London streets.

Slowly, she walked up the path leading to the elegant townhouse. The lavish architecture and lush gardens were nothing like the home Juliet had grown up in. Her father had been a vicar, and his house had been unadorned and simple. He hadn't believed that a person should live with so much luxury. Not that he faulted those that did have a more extravagant lifestyle. It was a matter of choice and beliefs. At least, that is what her father told her. She believed he'd convinced himself that fate had given him everything he needed so he could accept they were poor.

She was not so devout.

Juliet needed little. She hadn't been given every opportunity that other ladies had. But there were some necessities she could not go without. Basic things like food, shelter, and proper attire. She had none of those things. Well, that wasn't entirely true. Her attire could be considered proper even if it was old and ill fitting... No one would mistake her as a woman of ill-repute, and she certainly didn't have clothing befitting a rich man's mistress.

Though that position sounded more appealing by the day.

Finally, Juliet reached the front entrance. Juliet lifted her cold, stiff fingers and lifted the knocker, then rapped it twice against the large wood door. Another chilly wind racked through her entire body. Her teeth chattered as she waited for someone to open the door. She prayed it wouldn't be much longer. Surely someone was home. Had she made another mistake? She'd made so many and she couldn't afford another one.

The door opened and an older gentleman stood before her. He had pure white hair and bushy eyebrows that matched. His eyes were a watery blue and with fine lines in the corners. He stared at her for several moments before speaking. "How may I help you," he asked in a hoarse voice that seemed almost as weathered as the man himself.

"I'm here to see Lady Wyndam," she told him.

"Is she expecting you," he inquired. "Do you have a calling card?"

This was the hard part. The Dowager Countess of Wyndam wouldn't be expecting her. Why should she? She had been a good friend of her grandfather's and she prayed the countess could help her. Juliet needed work of some kind. She didn't expect charity. "I'm afraid I do not have a card," she said. "My name is Miss Juliet Adams. Could you please let her know I am here?"

The old man studied her and then opened the door wider. "Come inside out of the cold." Juliet entered and glanced around the foyer. It was as grand as the outside and she hadn't walked very far into the townhouse, and the warmth almost hurt against her frozen limbs. "Wait here," he told her. "I'll see if Lady Wyndam is at home to visitors."

He walked away and didn't glance back. The old man must trust she wouldn't try to steal anything or go anywhere she wasn't allowed to. Juliet rubbed her hands together and sighed. She couldn't remember the last time she'd been this warm. The small room she'd been able to let for the past week had provided none. It had thin walls and no hearth to light a fire in. The only thing it gave her was a small reprieve from the worst of the cold weather.

The butler came back to the foyer and met her gaze. "Please follow me," he said. "The countess will see you in her sitting room."

Juliet did as he ordered. It didn't take long for them to arrive at the countess's sitting room. They walked inside and the countess sat in a hair with an ornate cane in one of her hands. There was a fire burning in the hearth. The afternoon sun bathed the room in light through the large windows. She smiled at the butler and said, "Have tea and biscuits sent in. We will be a while."

"Yes, my lady," the butler said and left them alone.

Once he was gone, Lady Wyndam turned to her. "Come sit, girl. You look as if you haven't slept in days."

She had slept little. Juliet had been far too cold to properly rest, and her situation was enough to keep anyone from sleeping properly. "Yes, my lady," she replied, then sat on the settee across from her. "Thank you for seeing me."

Lady Wyndam narrowed her gaze. "You're Regina's daughter, aren't you?"

Her mother had been born Regina Jones, daughter of Baron Redcliffe. Her grandfather had died before she was born, and her mother had given her life by bringing Juliet into the world. "I am," she said.

"I thought so," she said. "Your father died a fortnight ago. Why are you not with your stepmother and younger sister?"

Juliet closed her eyes and took a deep breath. "My father's vicarage is being taken over by a new vicar and their family. He wasn't..." She took a moment to garner a bit of courage. "He didn't have much and we're quite poor. At least I am..."

"I see," Lady Wyndam said. "You need not say more. I understand completely." The countess sighed. "Your stepmother went to live with her father and took Clara with her." She tilted her head to the side. "You're eighteen now, are you not? She probably thought you're old enough to see to your own needs. Millicent has always been selfish, and honestly, she wouldn't care about Clara either if she could leave her to her own devices. It doesn't matter that she'd her daughter and you're not. That's never mattered to your stepmother."

"No, it hasn't." Her stepmother had always treated Clara and Juliet the same. Clara was with her now because she was the granddaughter of a viscount, and it was conditional she brought her home with her. Millicent's family would take care of her and her daughter, but her stepdaughter wasn't their concern. Her stepmother had come by her self-ishness honestly. "Lady Wyndam," Juliet began. "I need help finding a position. I need to be able to support myself. Will you help me?"

"Of course, dear," she said, then smiled. "And I have the perfect position for you."

"You do?" Was it really that easy? "What position?"

"You will be my companion and aide. I'm not as young as I used to be and I forget things." She tapped the side of her head. "You can help me remember what I should and live here with me. It will make my life much easier. Do you think you can do that?"

Juliet didn't believe for one second that Lady Wyndam was that forgetful. This was her way of making sure Juliet didn't end up on the streets. She wanted to say no and that she did not expect charity. However, she was no fool. This was position would save her life and she would be the best companion a lady could have. "I can," she said in a soft tone. "Thank you."

"Ah, here is the tea." A maid strolled in carrying a tray with the tea and biscuits. "Set it over there, Sarah. We can pour ourselves." The maid did as she was instructed, then left the room. "Now that we settled, you're to be my companion. It is time to discuss the rest of it. Tomorrow we will have my seamstress make you new gowns. You must be presentable when we are socializing. I'll also expect you to keep up my correspondence and social engagements."

"I can't..."

"Do not tell me you cannot accept the gowns. You need them and it is part of your position to look the part of a proper lady's companion. Consider it part of your salary." Lady Wyndam grinned. "This will not be an easy position. Take the benefits I'm offering you."

Juliet smiled. "Very well."

"Now pour us some tea and we will discuss the rest."

One day, Juliet hoped to be as strong willed and confident as Lady Wyndam. She owed the countess so much, and she hadn't really begun to be her companion. This had been her last hope, and somehow it had worked out better than she could ever have expected. She'd lost so much in a short time. Perhaps her life had finally taken a turn for the better...

Excerpt: Her Duke to Savor

WAYWARD DUKES' ALLIANCE

Prologue

Elias Stevens, the Marquess of Savorton, leaned back in his chair and rocked it on the back two legs as he studied his cards. How many should he discard? After pondering it for a few moments, he set his chair back down on all four legs and leaned on the table. He plucked five cards out of his hand and placed them face down on the table, and then drew five more from the deck.

He refrained from grinning at the cards he'd added to his hand. He glanced up at his dearest friend, Elena, the Dowager Countess of Dryden. Her dark red hair shimmered in the candlelight. She was studying her own cards. They were engrossed in a duel of sorts as they played a grueling game of piquet. This was their last hand in a set of six and would determine which one of them came out the winner. It was close and either of them might be declared the victor.

"It's your turn, love," Eli reminded her.

"I'm aware," she drawled. "I do not need your guidance." Elena winked. "I'm a far better player than you are."

"Debatable," he replied in an arrogant tone. "I am not so certain you're correct."

Her lips lifted into one of her sensual smiles. It was the type of smile that would set most men aflame with desire, but Eli felt nothing. For him that smile meant something far different. The minx was about to pounce and he would end up metaphorically wounded after she made her strike. Hell. She was going to win, and he didn't like it.

"You always did hate losing," she replied in a glib tone. She removed three cards from her hand and then replaced them with three more from the deck. "There's no need for deliberations. We both know the truth."

"That piquet is a game of chance?" Eli lifted a brow. "In that you are correct."

She laughed and then grinned at him. "I suppose that is true with any game used for the purpose of gambling. Luck may or may not be on your side."

She rearranged her card in her hand. "But we both know piquet is much more than that. It requires skill, strategy, and an excellent memory. I happen to have all three."

Eli shook his head and sighed and made his declarations, and they continued on with the game. After they were done playing, he had to admit, "I'm not saying you are better."

"Of course you will not. I'd expect nothing less." Her gray eyes sparkled with mischief. "You never have. Why would you change that core part of you now?"

They were at Elena's London townhouse. Many members of the ton believed they were lovers, but nothing could be farther from the truth. Elena and Eli had been friends since they were children. He was only three years older than her, and they first met when he was four and she could barely stand to walk in the nursery. Their mothers had been close and that had brought them together often. Eli was as protective of Elena as he would be if he'd had a sister. When she had married an old man, he had tried to persuade her against the match, but she reminded him they all had their duties to perform and her marriage landed firmly in that column. Her father had arranged the marriage, and she had done as she was told.

Elena had regretted it as her marriage made her miserable. Her husband hadn't been abusive, exactly, but he'd been cold. When she failed to conceive, he'd treated her as if she were a useless person. He may never have physically hit her, but his words were like blows that failed to leave a visible bruise. Eli had never been happier that a man died. When the Earl of Dryden dropped dead suddenly he had rejoiced, and secretly so had Elena.

"Do you think you'll ever remarry?" he asked.

She snorted. "Not bloody likely. One marriage of inconvenience is enough to turn me away from such an endeavor." Elena gathered the cards and stacked them neatly on the table. "Why do you ask?"

He didn't want to tell her he'd been thinking about how unhappy she had been. Elena enjoyed being a widow. She had freedom and if she wanted a lover, she could and probably had taken one. Eli didn't ask her about anything he didn't really want answers to. "What if you fell in love?"

"That is even more unlikely. Love is a myth they try to make a woman believe." She leaned back and studied him. "Are you in love, Eli?"

"Absolutely not," he said in an emphatic tone.

"Unless you count that gorgeous opera singer, I spent an evening with a few nights ago. She was delicious and might convince me I could believe in love."

He was far too busy helping build Savorton Shipping. His family had struggled when he was younger and now that he could, he worked to make their fortune something that rivaled even the most affluent in English society. He was an heir to a dukedom and now as well. His father had become frail in his old age and left running all the estates to Eli. He did not have time for love.

"A night of passion is not love," Elena replied in a dry tone. "Neither of us is on the market for that elusive emotion."

"So you do not believe you will ever willingly give your heart away?" This seemed like an opportunity. Should he take it? Elena had never really given any man a chance, and she had good reason for that. As a widow of wealthy means, she didn't have to remarry. "You don't have to marry a man if you love him, you know."

"I'm aware," she said, then tilted her head to the side. "I never have to marry again. But you do."

"I've never been married, love," he replied. "I cannot marry again when I never have."

"You are purposely misunderstanding me," she accused. "You know perfectly well what I meant. You're going to be a duke one day and you need heirs."

"I was hoping to convince you to marry me," he said in a glib tone. "You're the only woman I actually like."

"What a vile thing to suggest." She glared at him. "The very idea of sharing a bed with you..." Elena shuddered.

"Now that wasn't necessary. I'm not revolting." He frowned. She made a valid argument, though. Eli didn't wish to bed her any more than she wanted to be with him.

"Darling," she began. "You are passably handsome. I've heard many debutantes expound on your breathtaking visage. Apparently, your black hair and green eyes make them swoon with desire."

"Of course they desire to be a future duchess, and my gorgeous physique has nothing to do with their admiration." Eli might be a bit jaded. "I am not marrying until I absolutely have to, and love won't be part of the bargain."

"That's too bad," she said in a somber tone. "You're destined to have a marriage like mine."

"I won't be a brute like your husband was. I'd

never treat a woman so callously." He wouldn't. Eli had to believe he'd be better than the late Earl of Dryden. Elena was still young and only eight and twenty. She could find someone to be happy with. Somehow, he had to convince her to try.

"Perhaps not," she agreed. "You might be the one that is emotionally abused. I pray you choose wisely."

He smiled. "I'll have you approve of my future wife. You may have better judgement than me."

"I already do," she said, then laughed. "Perhaps we should make a wager."

It couldn't be that easy... She was playing right into his plans. Elena was a lot like him. She hated to lose. "What sort of wager?"

She tapped on the cards. "All gambling is a matter of chance, but some games are a little more than that. Much like piquet, love can be played in a similar fashion."

"So we use our strategy and skill to avoid fall-ing?" he asked, trying to understand her meaning.

"In a sense," she replied. "We will also have to keep track of all the players, for unlike our little game here, there will be more than two."

"And what exactly is this wager?" Eli asked.

"How about we make it simple," she began. "The

first to fall in love by the end of Christmastide loses and owes the other a boon."

He pondered her suggestion. "And what if neither of us falls?"

"Then we both win," she said in a wistful tone. "Or perhaps we will both lose, depending on one's perspective."

Eli doubted he would fall in love. He had yet to meet a woman that inspired such an insipid emotion in him. "All right, I accept. In fact, I have the perfect playing field for us."

She lifted a brow. "Oh?"

"Lady Winston is having a house party. It begins in a couple of weeks and will extend through the entirety of Christmastide. My mother has been hounding me to attend. I'll tell her I will as long as you go and we can put our wager to the test."

Elena steepled her fingers together. "Excellent," she said in a gleeful tone. "Let the best player win, then."

He was going to enjoy watching her fall, for he knew something she did not. The Earl of Northfield would be in attendance. Elena had never said as much, but the earl had been her first and only love. One she had never had a chance at having a rela-tionship with. Elena had shoved those feelings deep inside her and prepared to marry the Earl of Dryden as her father had ordered. Perhaps this was her second chance at finding happiness.

He wasn't worried about himself. Eli had time to find a suitable wife. His concern was for his dearest friend and helping her find a love she deserved. Besides he hadn't lied, Eli didn't believe in love, at least not when it came to his own life. Love was for other people. Individuals who had the luxury of accepting that gift into their lives. Eli would never be that fortunate.

About Dawn Brower

USA TODAY Bestselling author, DAWN BROWER writes both historical and contemporary romance. There are always stories inside her head; she just never thought she could make them come to life. That creativity has finally found an outlet.

Growing up, she was the only girl out of six children. She raised two boys as a single mother; there is never a dull moment in her life. Reading books is her favorite hobby, and she loves all genres.

www.authordawnbrower.com
TikTok: @1DawnBrower

BB bookbub.com/authors/dawn-brower
f facebook.com/1DawnBrower
X x.com/1DawnBrower
instagram.com/1DawnBrower
g goodreads.com/dawnbrower

Also by Dawn Brower

HISTORICAL

Stand alone:

Broken Pearl

A Wallflower's Christmas Kiss

A Gypsy's Christmas Kiss

Marsden Romances

A Flawed Jewel

A Crystal Angel

A Treasured Lily

A Sanguine Gem

A Hidden Ruby

A Discarded Pearl

Marsden Descendants

Rebellious Angel

Tempting An American Princess

How to Kiss a Debutante

Loving an America Spy

Ever Beloved

Forever My Earl

Always My Viscount

Infinitely My Marquess

Eternally My Duke

Bluestockings Defying Rogues

When An Earl Turns Wicked

A Lady Hoyden's Secret

One Wicked Kiss

Earl In Trouble

All the Ladies Love Coventry

One Less Scandalous Earl

Confessions of a Hellion

The Vixen in Red

Lady Pear's Duke

Scandal Meets Love

Love Only Me (Amanda Mariel)

Find Me Love (Dawn Brower)

If It's Love (Amanda Mariel)

Odds of Love (Dawn Brower)

Believe In Love (Amanda Mariel)

Chance of Love (Dawn Brower)

Love and Holly (Amanda Mariel)

Love and Mistletoe (Dawn Brower

The Neverhartts

Never Defy a Vixen

Never Disregard a Wallflower

Never Dare a Hellion

Never Deceive a Bluestocking

Never Disrespect a Governess

Never Desire a Duke

Lady Be Wicked/Wayward Dukes'/Wicked Widows'

Her Rogue for One Night (Wicked Widows)

A Lady Never Tells

Her Duke of Sin (Wayward Dukes')

Her Duke to Savor (Wayward Dukes')

Coming in 2024/2025

A Lady Never Confesses

A Lady Never Forgets

Her Rogue for Christmas (Wicked Widows)

Her Rogue to Kiss Good Morning (Wicked Widows)

Begin Again

There You'll Be

Better as a Memory

Won't Let Go

Heart's Intent

One Heart to Give

Unveiled Hearts

Heart of the Moment

Kiss My Heart Goodbye

Heart in Waiting

Heart Lessons

A Heart Redeemed

Kismet Bay

Once Upon a Christmas

New Year Revelation

All Things Valentine

Luck At First Sight

Endless Summer Days

A Witch's Charm

All Out of Gratitude

Christmas Ever After